YOURS,
FOR A PRYCE

BRENDA BARRETT

JAMAICA
TREASURES

Yours, For A Pryce

A Jamaica Treasures Book/December 2019
Published by Jamaica Treasures
Kingston, Jamaica

This is a work of fiction. Names, characters, places, and incidents are either the product of the author's imagination or are used fictitiously. Any resemblance to an actual person or persons, living or dead, events, or locales is entirely coincidental.

978-976-8247-72-8
Jamaica Treasures
P.O. Box 482
Kingston 19
Jamaica W.I.
www.fiwibooks.com

ALSO BY BRENDA BARRETT

FULL CIRCLE
NEW BEGINNINGS
THE PREACHER AND THE PROSTITUTE
AFTER THE END
THE EMPTY HAMMOCK
THE PULL OF FREEDOM
REBOUND SERIES
THREE RIVERS SERIES
NEW SONG SERIES
BANCROFT SERIES
MAGNOLIA SISTERS SERIES
SCARLETT SERIES
WILEY BROTHERS SERIES
PRYCE SISTERS SERIES

ABOUT THE AUTHOR

Books have always been a big part of life for Jamaican born Brenda Barrett, she reports that she gets withdrawal symptoms if she does not consume at least two books per week. That is all she can manage these days, as her days are filled with writing, a natural progression from her love of reading. Currently, Brenda has several novels on the market, she writes predominantly in the historical fiction, Christian fiction, comedy and romance genres.

Apart from writing fictional books, Brenda writes for her blogs blackhair101.com; where she gives hair care tips and fiwibooks.com, where she shares about her writing life.

You can connect with Brenda online at:
Brenda-Barrett.com
Twitter.com/AuthorWriterBB
Facebook.com/AuthorBrendaBarrett

Chapter One

"So Tiana is engaged and has just finished writing a miniseries. Giselle finished the diamond league at the top of her event and uninjured," Sharla looked at Elsa with a smile, "and you are bored and unemployed."

"That's about right." Elsa glared at her aunt. "Thanks for the recap. Welcome to the first episode of the lousiest Pryce Triplet."

Sharla laughed. "Even in your doldrums, you manage to add some creativity and humor to the conversation."

"This is no laughing matter, Aunt Sharla," Elsa groaned. "I am the only of my sisters that is unlucky in love, unlucky in employment and just plain unlucky."

"I am not worried about you." Sharla sipped her drink slowly. "You will land on your feet."

"How?" Elsa growled. "I applied to all the advertising agencies in Kingston, every single one, including Magnus Communication, and I swore I wouldn't apply to them. I even went to Toddy with hat in hand, begging for him to use his connections."

"And?" Sharla asked.

"And nothing…" Elsa widened her eyes. "Nothing at all. I can't believe Geo King is so powerful that he could blacklist me so thoroughly. I had a small hope that because I knew Mason, I could get a foot in at his company, but even there, I have no luck."

"Mason Magnus?" Sharla asked. "I can't believe you applied, and he said no."

"I don't know if he knows I applied to them. His company is huge and has an HR department." Elsa heaved a deep sigh. "I sent my résumé through the regular channels. I felt kind of weird applying in the first place, especially since he has a vendetta with Toddy."

"But not you," Sharla said shrewdly. "Mason likes you."

"No, he doesn't," Elsa snorted. "He has called me a wild cat, an untamed shrew, an untamable slip of a girl who will do anything for thrills. That's what he said within my hearing. Can you imagine what he says when I am not around?"

Sharla grinned. "And what did you call him in return?"

"Boring, bug-eyed twerp, creep psychopath," Elsa sighed, "and plenty more. We have known each other for years. He makes me uncomfortable."

"Why?" Sharla got up and headed to the kitchen.

"Because…" Elsa shrugged, "I don't know. When Toddy was married to his mom he would sometimes come over for the weekends, but he was silent for most of the time, which was creepy. Sometimes I would catch him looking at me. He doesn't do it to anybody else. He'd just sit and look at me, not Giselle, not Tiana. Me."

"And I say again he liked you or was fascinated with you." Sharla looked in the fridge. "Why do you have so much take out?"

"Went to a party at the Waterfalls," Elsa grunted. "There was more food than people."

"Okay," Sharla rummaged around in the fridge and finally pulled out a container. "If you really wanted a job, you'd call Mason, take advantage of his fascination."

"He is not fascinated with me. Not the way you think." Elsa snorted. "What I didn't tell you was that I was extremely mean to him in the past. I did stuff to make him react."

"Like what?" Sharla put the dish in the microwave and turned to Elsa. "Whatever could you have done?"

"I, er," Elsa looked away shyly. "I used to...I haven't told anyone this."

"What?" Sharla asked, "what on earth did you do to poor Mason?"

"I would strip for him, dance while I was doing it, and then one time I kind of...well, I knew he was watching, and I can't say it out loud. Let's just say I was naked, and I knew he was sneaking around upstairs. I pleasured myself gave him an eyeful with lots of noise and then..."

"Then what? Sharla gasped.

"He stopped coming by the house after that. I think I broke him."

"Suppose he had raped you?" Sharla had a horrified expression on her face, "How old were you?"

"Sixteen." Elsa sighed. "Or fifteen, what does it matter?"

"What does it matter?" Sharla widened her eyes. "You can't egg a man on like that. What on earth possessed you?"

"Myrna said he was a virgin and was waiting for marriage. I couldn't believe it. He is a man. In my experience, men don't wait for marriage. I am more used to Toddy's kind of man. You know, loads of women all the time. So I wanted to test Mason to see if it were true."

"Good Lord, help my wayward niece," Sharla said dramatically.

"He passed the test." Elsa frowned. "Maybe he doesn't have anything down there. Maybe he is a eunuch. Maybe he lost his thing in an accident. Or maybe he is impotent. Have you thought of that?"

The microwave pinged, announcing that it had finished the cycle. Sharla ignored it and shook her head. "No, I haven't thought of that, Elsa Cara Pryce…"

"Don't worry about it," Elsa waved off her aunt. "I cured him of staring at me like a zombie. He doesn't look me in the eyes anymore, and I think he avoids me at all cost. Three months ago, I went to the industry thing, where Geo King, my boss, tried to kiss me, and I broke his nose."

Sharla sighed. "You are lucky Geo didn't press charges."

"I wish he had," Elsa snarled, "then we could have the true story out there. I really hate the one he has been telling people… that I came on to him blah blah blah. All boring and untrue.

"Anyway, Mason gave a good talk, and I know he saw me. I went close to him to say hello, and he blanked me, the twerp.

"Though I can't call him a twerp anymore. He has changed. You should see him now. He has grown into his looks. He is, and I am going to reluctantly say this, looking good. He gives me a Lance Gross kind of vibe."

"I can't believe what you did," Sharla still looked shocked. "What kind of behavior was that? You better thank God it was Mason, a principled man, and not anyone else."

"We all do stupid things when we were younger." Elsa sighed, "I can't take it back now. It was nearly ten years ago. Now I just want to be employed. I may just be desperate enough to call Mason about hiring me."

****

"Hello, darling," Mason sighed in relief when he heard his mother's voice. She didn't sound down or ill. His secretary had said the call was urgent.

"Mom." He adjusted his tone to that of a loving son, a point that was not lost on the people sitting around the conference table. He had just been in full boss mode, after demanding that they find a solution to take some of the work off his hands. He had too much work to do, and one of their most significant accounts wanted to work only with him.

His mother had killed the momentum, his staff had been giving him some good suggestions about his dilemma, but she was forgiven. Celine Magnus Pryce would always be forgiven.

"I don't want to keep you, but I have a little favor to ask," Celine said briskly.

"Anything." Mason swung his chair to avoid the eyes of the two men and one woman who was listening keenly to his side of the conversation.

"Elsa Pryce, she wants to be a...a...I don't know... something in advertising. You own an advertising firm, hire her."

"Hellcat Elsa!" He almost hissed the no that was at the tip of his tongue.

Instead, he cleared his throat. Whatever he said about Elsa had to be a private conversation. He didn't want Elsa in his building, in his offices, or near him. There was something about her that drove him slightly crazy.

She could effortlessly make his blood pressure rise, and she had the uncanny ability to stick in his skin like a burr. Nobody else had that effect on him.

"Mason," Celine insisted, "just hire the girl. I can hear you mind formulating arguments as to why you shouldn't, but she was your favorite triplet at one time, remember?"

Mason sighed. Unfortunately, his mother knew exactly why Elsa had been his favorite triplet. She even knew about his most recent run-in with Elsa. His mother knew their mortifying secret.

"That was in the past." Mason murmured. He didn't want his colleagues to know what he was talking about. He had to be as cryptic as possible.

"She sent her résumé to your offices," Celine said chirpily. "Find it and hire her as a favor to me."

"What if she is a complete disaster?" Mason asked.

"Then fire her," Celine said. "I will not interfere then, but from all accounts, I heard Elsa was very good at her previous job."

Mason sighed. "I will look into it."

He hung up the phone and swung around to his directors. "Where were we?"

"We were discussing your workload." Paxton Hill, his HR Manager said, "and I was saying that we would have to hire new staff, there is no getting around it. We already did some hires for the upcoming holidays, and even then, we are going to have to do some things out of the house to keep up with the workload."

"That's true," Owen his advertising manager added. "We are working on a bunch of political ads for the various bi-elections coming up, we are swimming with the Christmas season stuff, and along with our regular customers, all our resources are tapped out. We need new people, and we need them fast. People who can hit the ground running, preferably multi-skilled persons."

"Because we can't turn away business." Emma, his

accounts manager, pointed out. "Those new accounts you have coming in have large budgets with the potential for even more business in the future."

"Okay." Mason nodded. "Paxton, go-ahead and hire more people as you see fit. I will find someone to deal with these myself. He tapped the two files on his desk. We need a special projects manager. Someone efficient, someone who will report to me, someone I will work closely with because I can't handle anything else right now, not with Edmond Greyson breathing down my neck and all the advertising firms on this side of the planet competing to represent him for his newest acquisitions. I need to focus on his account exclusively."

Emma nodded. "That's more like it."

"Okay, let's get cracking, I know you are busy people," Mason stood up. "Paxton, I want to speak to you about a résumé."

Everyone filed out except for Paxton.

Mason had inherited Paxton from Pryceless Advertising, Toddy Pryce's company. When the two departments had merged, Paxton had become his HR Manager. He had the experience, and the qualifications and Mason liked working with him.

They also had tenuous family ties, if you could call it that. Paxton's mother, Noreen, had been Toddy's third wife, and his mother Celine the fourth. They both were a part of Toddy's legions of stepchildren.

"Do you have a résumé from Elsa Pryce?" Mason asked.

"Yes," Paxton nodded. "I put it in file thirteen, never to see the light of day again."

"Why?" Mason asked.

Paxton shifted in his seat uncomfortably. "Well, there are the rumors…"

"The rumors about her and Geo King?" Mason raised an eyebrow. "I am sure that is rubbish, Elsa may be many things but chasing Geo King and assaulting him when he declined her advances does not ring as true. Elsa doesn't chase men, they chase her."

"I know, right?" Paxton smiled. "Toddy's triplet sisters have grown into beautiful women. I figured Geo's interpretation of the incident wasn't true. I don't think anyone believes it. I just thought that you wouldn't want her to work here. She is a Pryce after all, Toddy Pryce's favorite little sister. I heard the rumors that you wanted to take Toddy down. I just thought…"

"That I wouldn't want her here?" Mason snorted, there was some truth to that. He didn't want Elsa as a visible reminder that there was some good in Toddy Pryce. He had taken in his orphaned sisters without blinking an eye, and he also didn't want Elsa around to remind him about what happened between them four years ago.

"When I worked for Toddy," Paxton cleared his throat, "he went on and on about Elsa taking over from him, Elsa being as smart as a whip, Elsa had the advertising genes."

"I may not have a choice now about any of this." Mason got up and started pacing the conference room. "My mother says I should hire her, and the purpose of the meeting just now was that we needed extra staff."

Paxton chuckled. "Quite the coincidence."

Mason looked at him sharply. "Yes, it is, almost as if it were orchestrated."

"I don't have those kinds of powers Mason," Paxton protested, "I couldn't command your mother to call at the same time that we have a genuine staff shortage."

Mason grunted and stared broodingly outside the window.

"So, what are you going to have her do?" Paxton asked.

"I need someone to do the ad campaign for Ace and Quade Jackson's newest business. They inherited their uncle's luxury retirement home complex," Mason said contemplatively. "I'll put Elsa in charge of it."

"That's huge!" Paxton exclaimed. "So are you making her your special projects manager?"

"Yes." Mason nodded. "She can handle it. I kept an eye on her, tracked her career from the moment she started working. I was not surprised that she was made an assistant advertising manager in two years. King was an idiot for letting her go."

"Oh," Paxton opened his mouth. "If I knew you felt that way, I would have hired her in the last batch of new hires, we could use somebody like her."

"I thought about it before my mother's interference, just didn't think I could work with her. Elsa and I have a turbulent history."

Mason leaned his head on the glass and watched the sea below. He had moved to the waterfront area in downtown Kingston after buying and renovating one of the historic buildings. On the seventh floor where his office was, they had an unfettered view of mountains to the north and the sea to the south. He could look at whatever view stirred his creativity.

He had the sudden urge not to just look but to participate. He wished he could leave the office and swim in the sparkling blue waters below or hike in the Blue Mountains.

If only he had the time, he could drive to the north coast where he had a beach house and just stay there for the week or take some time off to stay at his mountain home. He only went home to Hibiscus Lodge on the weekends these days. His city apartment was where he spent the majority of his time on the weekdays. Such a pity, his home in the mountains was a perfect getaway.

He was driving himself too hard. Maybe he was even working himself into an early grave.

"Mason?" Paxton said beside him, "you zoned out of the conversation."

"I am tired," Mason confessed. "I've been burning the candle at both ends."

"I know." Paxton nodded. "You should give up a couple of the things you have on your plate. You are so busy it makes me tired just watching you."

"My father did all of this with ease," Mason said wearily. "He was a good father, a perfect husband, a senator, a business owner, and he sat on several boards."

"Didn't he die from a heart attack at fifty? Paxton frowned, "and wasn't he so busy that he lost his company to Toddy Pryce?"

Mason sighed. "He lost everything to Toddy Pryce."

"And you got everything back before you were thirty." Paxton looked out at the scenery, "but at what cost? You are too tired to even enjoy it."

Mason looked at him sharply. "Has my mother been talking to you?"

"I talk to Celine all the time, but your name rarely comes up, this was just a casual observation," Paxton shrugged. "You don't have fun. You don't have a life. You are the first one here and the last one out. You need to feed your soul, slow down, read a book, listen to some uplifting music, go to church."

"You do sound like my mother." Mason laughed dryly. "The last time she told me to feed my soul, I went to her church, and they incorporated my help to head a fund-raising committee. I was very good at it too."

"Maybe you should just take some quiet time away from people," Paxton murmured. "You are obviously an overachiever, and you cannot take it easy. All of this high-octane living will come crashing down on your head one day."

"That is not bad advice," Mason swiped his hand over his eyes. "I forget what it was like to be young and carefree without the world pressing on my shoulders."

"I unwind with my children," Paxton said. "I can't imagine life without them. At the end of the day, they force me to slow down to relive that innocence."

"Children." Mason grimaced. "In my book there first has to be a wife. How is yours by the way?"

"Good." Paxton grinned. "She is quite concerned about you since your breakup with Anna Kay. She thought you would have made a connection with her friend Kelly at her birthday party."

"Good heavens, no," Mason groaned. "I couldn't stand the constant need to fill every silence with inane conversation. That is the one thing Anna Kay had going for her, she wasn't overly chatty."

Paxton chuckled. "I told her. I said Mason has a specific type. She can't be talkative or too silent or adventurous or mousy or…"

"Oh, stop it," Mason growled. "I am not that picky."

"You are going to be a lifelong bachelor, Paxton mused. "I guess we all have to accept that and accept you for who you are."

"I would get married," Mason said contemplatively. "I am not anti-marriage, nor do I particularly like being single. I have serious doubts though, that the person I have in mind wants that kind of thing."

"Oh, really?" Paxton tried to temper his interest, but it didn't come off right, "I didn't know you have someone in mind."

"The fantasy girl," Mason chuckled. "I think most people have a fantasy person or an ideal. My fantasy girl is vastly different from me, I think we are opposites in every way. I don't know if we could ever work, and I am not inclined to try. I don't want to destroy the illusion and let real life intrude. So I stay away from her keep her and my fantasies to myself."

"But that's no way to live!" Paxton said, appalled. "Real life is passing you by. You are thirty-two years old, how old is this girl, woman?"

"In her twenties." Mason didn't want to go into specifics. He didn't want Paxton to know who his fantasy girl was. "But you have a point, Paxton. I am getting tired of living like this, especially after I read about her in the papers with yet another man. Maybe I should take my chance with her and shatter the illusion."

Mason looked at Paxton and smiled faintly. "Could you email me Elsa's résumé?"

"Sure thing," Paxton nodded. "You sure you don't want me to interview her instead?"

"Quite sure." Mason nodded. "As special projects manager she and I will work together. I have to see if we are compatible. If not, I will hand her off to your department."

Chapter Two

"**E**verything is going according to your plan." Paxton slid into the seat across from Toddy in the semi-dark sports bar. "I sat on the résumé as you requested. Today, Celine finally called Mason and asked him to give Elsa a job, just as you said she would."

"I know." Toddy chuckled. "Sharla called me and asked me for Celine's number."

"Sharla is Elsa's aunt?" Paxton asked.

"Yes, the mother hen for the girls, always telling me what to do with them." Toddy nodded. "She would flip if she knew I have been busy calling in favors to block Elsa getting a job even though everybody wants to get Elsa on their team."

"You are shrewd," Paxton chuckled. "I doubted that this would work out like you said."

"Elsa thought it was because of the Geo King incident why no one wanted to hire her." Toddy laughed. "I actually went to his office and threatened to castrate him, both literally and figuratively, if he said anything bad about her or thought to bring charges. I protect my own."

"That's what big brothers are for," Paxton nodded approvingly.

"Elsa would kill me if she finds out that I blacklisted her, but I wanted her at Magnus Communications, and I wanted her to work with Mason."

"She'll never know." Paxton nodded. "At least she'll never hear it from me. I can assure you of that."

"I know." Toddy looked at Paxton proudly. "You were, and always will be one of my favorite stepsons."

Paxton laughed. "Better than Mason?"

"Oh goodness, yes." Toddy muttered. "I don't know what I did to that young man to make him hate me so much. He blames me for his father's heart attack, for losing the house he grew up in, and for marrying his mother. And he has been after me like a hunter. I feel like prey."

"How close is he to taking your senate seat?" Paxton asked concerned.

"By law, my seat is for the life of the parliament. I cannot be fired until parliament is dissolved. Unless, they find that I did something criminal or unethical," Toddy sighed, "then I can be pressured to resign. I heard that Mason is digging into my past business dealings."

"But you haven't done anything criminal or illegal," Paxton said loyally.

"No," Toddy shook his head, "not really. I may have invested in a business that would fail the smell test. I didn't have anything to do with it directly, but I was a shareholder, a sleeping partner until three years ago. I pulled out of it when it was safely in the black."

"Oh," Paxton relaxed in his chair. "Which business is that?"

"Camden Howard's nightclub," Toddy said heavily.

"You mean Jaded Night Club?" Paxton widened his eyes, "Oh my."

"He is family," Toddy sighed. "He is my nephew, my brother, Peter's boy. Peter did not claim him though. He had a rough life growing up without his father, so when he came to me for a loan to start that business, I was happy to help. He had just come out of rehab, nobody in the family would give him the time of day, except me. He made a success of the place, and I am proud of him."

"Toddy," Paxton said, looking around before whispering, "they are investigating that nightclub, for being a human trafficking hub."

"I know." Toddy sighed, "Camden says he is cooperating with the police and that he didn't know anything about the seedier side of what is going on. After all, he doesn't do the day to day running of the place anymore, but that doesn't matter, what do you think the headlines are going to say when they hear that I was involved?"

Paxton shrugged. "Senator Pryce Head of Human Trafficking Ring?"

"Or, Senator Invests in Exploiting Children for Sex." Toddy shook his head, "I just need to appear to have a tenuous link to this foolishness, and I am toast. My reputation, my investments with others, they will start treating me like a pariah. I might as well curl up in a corner and die."

"No," Paxton shook his head, "you can't think like that. Maybe they won't find any links to you and the nightclub. Maybe Mason won't dig up that piece of information."

"You clearly have no idea who I am dealing with here." Toddy snorted. "Mason Magnus wants my senate seat and he is very much interested in destroying me piece by piece. He has Cameron Grindley on my trail."

"The political fixer?" Paxton raised an eyebrow.

"The dirt digger, reputation destroyer, crazy manipulator," Toddy snorted. "Yup, him. And he'll find a link to me and that nightclub and then that's it. I am toast. I am finished in this town. Even if they find nothing at that nightclub when Cameron is done, the insinuations and whisperings that this news will generate will be force me to resign my senate seat. I will be talked about in every village and town in Jamaica. I will be ruined."

Paxton looked into Toddy's eyes; he was feeling genuinely disturbed.

"If it is any consolation," Paxton said soothingly, "Mason looks like he is very tired of the chase. Today he said as much."

"No, he is not." Toddy snorted. "He is one track-minded and determined. I have never met anyone as stubborn and determined as him, not even his father, Manuel Magnus, and that's saying a lot because Manuel was crazy. He was like a dog with a well-loved bone."

Paxton caressed the side of his glass, his mind racing. "You have to get in front of this before Cameron Grindley."

"I have thought of that," Toddy nodded, "but Camden asked me not to say anything yet. He swears there is nothing there, and he doesn't want me speaking about it and sullying his and the business' reputation. He says the law will vindicate him, and I believe him."

Paxton nodded. "That might be a miscalculation."

"It might be," Toddy tapped his fingers on the table, "I have to get Mason distracted; I have to do something to get him off my trail. So far, I've tried everything, I pleaded with his mother, he usually listens to her, but he still blames me for us breaking up, so that didn't work."

Paxton cleared his throat. "Didn't she catch you cheating?"

"That was years ago," Toddy said tiredly. "She has moved on, and she is happy, we are even on good terms. I am on good terms with all my exes, including your mother. I have never had a stepchild come after me like Mason has."

"You two have a convoluted past," Paxton murmured, "but I must admit, I am not sure why Mason is so determined to take you down."

"I don't know either," Toddy raised his hand for a waiter and ordered them drinks. "He decided that his father was done some injustice, and I am the villain. It is ironic, Manuel Magnus and I were good friends in the early years, we built our business together."

When the drinks came, he took a sip and grimaced. It was too sour. "I practically handed over my share of the company to Mason, and I didn't put up much of a fight when he offered through his development company to buy my house.

"He knows I love being a politician, and he is hell-bent on taking that away from me too. Elsa is my last hope to get him to see sense."

"How?" Paxton raised an eyebrow. "Of the three girls, you are choosing the most headstrong, the one least likely to do your bidding. She is a wild card. I thought you were an ad man, not a magician. Besides, he said he has a fantasy girl."

"Elsa is his fantasy girl." Toddy relaxed in his seat. "I know this for sure. I have my sources."

"He also said he would not pursue his fantasy because they are different in every way." Paxton cleared his throat. "I don't know about this, Toddy. When Mason makes up his mind about not doing something, he doesn't budge."

"I know," Toddy grinned, "but I orchestrated the first hurdle without a hitch. He will hire Elsa. She will be in his vicinity, and he will fall for her. How could he not? She is fun and adventurous and friendly and loyal and perfect for him. His fantasy girl.

"When he is well and truly hooked, I will offer him, Elsa, if he leaves me alone."

"Offer him Elsa?" Paxton laughed. "Maybe this is not one of your better plans, Toddy."

"Or maybe it is my most brilliant yet." Toddy held up his glass and clinked it to Paxton's. "Of the three girls Elsa is most loyal to me. Elsa has always sought my approval and my attention. We will see how this plays out."

Chapter Three

Elsa stepped into Magnus Communications, and could see her reflection in the glass above the receptionist area. She was in black leggings, black sneakers, and a bright yellow t-shirt that had the words, 'cute but psycho' splashed on the front. The place was empty. What she assumed would be a busy lobby was eerily quiet. She admired the black and white lobby area with the large Magnus Communications letters splashed in red above where the receptionist desk was.

The security guard who let her in paused while she looked around.

"Mr. Magnus is on the seventh floor, the office at the end. He is expecting you," The security guard said.

Elsa nodded. "Thank you."

He looked at her shirt, solemnly. "We have security on that floor as well. I'll tell them to be on the alert."

"For goodness sakes, it's just a t-shirt," Elsa growled. "I am not psycho."

"Then you shouldn't announce such a message to the world. Somebody will take you seriously." The guard still had not cracked a smile.

Elsa rolled her eyes and headed to the bank of elevators. She wondered if everybody at the company was ordered to suppress their humor like the boss.

Elsa pulled the headband from around her hair and ran her fingers through the curls, hoping to fluff it up a bit, it needed a trim. She hated her hair being more than three inches long. She bit her lips to give them some color. She had been on her way to the gym when Mason had called her phone.

Without preamble, he had asked her if she could come for a job interview.

"I was heading to the gym," Elsa had groaned. "It is eight-thirty at night. Who works at this unholy time?"

"Come as you are, Elsa. I can't fit this into my schedule for the rest of the week, and I would like to get this over with."

She had felt the urge to hang up the phone. She hated that he made her feel like a charity case.

She knew Sharla had called Celine. She didn't know that the response would be so swift. She had envisioned going to a job interview dressed to the nines, looking like she had just stepped out of a photoshoot. She would draw on her cat-eye makeup and walk through the lobby like she was on a runway and have Mason gasp in awe when he saw her.

Instead, she was looking a tad grubby. After all, she didn't wear makeup to the gym. She didn't care how she looked when she got there. She would sweat it all off anyway.

She could never understand the women who went to the gym to exercise with a full face of makeup. She went to the place to sweat, and a good cardio session would melt even waterproof makeup away. She usually didn't wear matching gym wear either. It was a coincidence that tonight her leggings and her sneakers were the same color.

She headed to the elevator and punched in for the seventh floor. She straightened her spine when she got inside and inhaled and exhaled deeply. She was feeling nervous. It was Mason she was going to face. Mason who had the power to make her feel gauche and uncertain about herself. He was the only man who wielded that power over her.

When she was younger, she had done and said the most outrageous things around him because he was so self-contained and distant. She had always wanted to break down that barrier, but had never managed to ruffle him, not even once. That irked her.

He was the one person she could not charm, the one man who didn't melt when she smiled or seemed susceptible to anything she did.

He called her names when she called him names, and he would sit and stare at her, not initiating any conversation with her. She was the one who would babble to him, telling him all of the things that she got up to. Even things that she hadn't told her sisters, all to get a rise out of him. And he had never blinked. Until that glitch in time four years ago.

She had never told anyone about, and she never would. It had been their secret, and it would remain their secret forever. She had told him then that she would never work for him. And now here she was, a charity case. She will have to be polite and professional and respectful.

He should be savoring this. He was probably waiting inside his office, ready to preach to her in his proper, staid way. That is what he did when he deigned to talk to her in the past, preach. He would make a good pastor.

She clutched her cavernous bag closer to her body and closed her eyes. Until four years ago, she had never heard Mason raise his voice or show any emotion.

Nine years before, when she had played Tina Turner's Private Dancer and stripped for him down to her panties, he hadn't batted an eyelash.

She had stopped teasing him in frustration then and told him he was an alien. He had responded that she was a provocative oversexed girl who was testing the boundaries of her female power.

And he had said it with no expression, just looking at her with the light glinting off his glasses. Mason's face was the definition of a poker-faced. She had only seen him genuinely smile for his mother.

He laughed and talked with Celine, and he was pleasant to Giselle and Tiana too. Especially Tiana, who had taken up the role of public defender whenever Elsa criticized him.

But Mason hadn't always been an emotionless zombie, had he? She had seen a sliver of a crack in his armor.

She didn't want to remember the details now. Not after all these years. She had flippantly given Sharla a tiny bit of the story about her younger years. It made her uncomfortable to explore, even in her own mind, what happened between her and Mason recently. Four years was recent, wasn't it?

She dragged her thoughts back to the present and willed herself to stay right here. She shouldn't be thinking about their secret, right before a showdown with Mason.

She hoped he had forgotten it too. God, please let him forget. She prayed feverishly. But knowing Mason, he wouldn't forget or forgive. How much had Celine had to beg for him to take her on?

She stepped onto the seventh floor and headed down the hallway. He was not the only one working, there were other office lights on. She passed a conference room with a group of people in there. Two persons were passionately arguing and gesturing at an idea board. She paused at the door. They had an audience of five, one of the spectators, a guy who looked vaguely familiar, waved to her, and she waved back.

She stepped away. She knew why he was familiar; he had acted in an advertisement that she had produced.

It made her nostalgic. Four months out in the ad world wilderness. She realized that she didn't want to do anything else; she loved the advertising world. She loved seeing a concept coming together. She loved getting a kernel of an idea and then putting on paper and then selling it to the client. She especially loved it when they liked the idea, and then she could start working on it.

She couldn't mess up this interview with Mason. She wanted back in.

She had been an assistant advertising manager when she worked at King Advertising, she wondered what position Mason was thinking of putting her in. He probably wanted to punish her for her past transgressions by giving her the most menial job.

She would take it, whatever it was. She wanted the opportunity to work here. It was the largest and best firm in Jamaica.

She didn't have to ask where Mason's office was. There was a large glassed off area where she assumed his secretary occupied. The blinds were opened, and she could see straight ahead to the lights out at sea.

"What a view for work!" She whistled. It stopped her in her tracks. "It must be an awesome view in the day."

"It is nice, isn't it?" Mason said behind her. "It's the same view from my apartment. As I recall, you gushed over that too."

Shots fired. He brought up the apartment.

She spun around. She hadn't heard him approach. She should have smelled him, though. He smelled good. She recognized the scent; he had always worn it. And she always gravitated to men who smelled like him. She slammed down that wayward thought and looked him over in what she hoped was a discrete manner.

He was dressed casually in jeans and a navy-blue muscle shirt. She hadn't expected that. She had envisioned him to be in a suit and a tie and looking like a stern school principal for what in his view would be an odious interview.

But tonight he didn't look uptight. He looked less wound up and more relaxed.

She cataloged his features quickly. He had the same dark skin, straight nose, impossibly white teeth, and reddish-pink lips, which were only emphasized by the darkness of his skin.

His body was muscular. He wasn't huge, but it was noticeable that he worked out. He was sporting a new, cleanly shaven hairstyle and a circular beard.

He was staring back at her, and she could clearly see his eyes through his glasses; they were a deep brown, almost black and magnetic.

She had trouble dragging hers from his. It reminded her of the first time she saw him. He had taken off his bulky Steve Urkel glasses and she had thought his eyes were pulling her in.

It had been a weird feeling then. It had made her uncomfortable. She had been relieved when he had put the glasses back on. But now he wasn't wearing glasses that could obscure his eyes and make them appear like bugs. These ones were barely there, and she could clearly see that he was staring at her in his usual unbothered, laser-focused manner. And she was feeling weird again.

This was an unfamiliar Mason Magnus. He looked even better than when she had seen him at the beginning of the summer at the Advertising Event in Negril. When had Mason gotten so swoon-worthy? He was looking better with age. It was usually the other way around for some people.

"You are looking gorgeous!" Elsa said out loud. "Like really good."

"Thank you," Mason said, his expression not changing. "You are not looking bad yourself Elsa. I like that hairstyle on you, it highlights your cheekbones. My office is that way."

He hooked his finger in the direction of his office.

Efficient and no-nonsense as usual, Elsa thought. She hadn't even told him hello when she declared that he was gorgeous. Stupid girl.

Mason's office was large. He had the same lovely view. He had pulled away the blinds to reveal the view. A circular conference table was at one end, and a large desk which looked squeaky clean with only a laptop in the middle was at the other end. The office was painted in a tranquil beige color, and a couple of framed advertising jobs were scattered throughout, along with his accolades and certificates and advertising trophies.

"Please have a seat," he indicated to one of the chairs across from his desk. "I am sorry to call you out so late. I know the time is unconventional for an interview, but I'll be busy for the rest of the week."

Elsa nodded. "It's fine. I am just happy for the opportunity to be considered for a position in advertising again."

"Why did you leave?" Mason steepled his fingers and trained his eyes on her.

"I... erm, my boss came on to me. I accidentally broke his nose and was fired instantly."

Mason just stared at her after she said that. He probably didn't believe her.

"I didn't provoke him," Elsa felt compelled to say. "I know

you, and I have…well me…I provoked you in the past, but this was totally different."

"Okay," Mason sat back in his chair. "Thank you for clearing that up. Tell me about the ad campaigns you did for King Advertising."

"I did quite a few," Elsa said in relief. He wasn't interested in talking about her past behavior with Geo King or seemed as if he cared one way or the other if she had really broken his nose, and he certainly didn't seem too bothered about their past.

She relaxed a little and began to talk.

Mason was a good listener. He asked her a question or two and watched as she handled it.

"Here is a situational question for you," Mason said after a while. "I give you a five million budget to do an advertising campaign for a retirement community. What would you do?"

"Is there any other information I can use?" Elsa frowned.

"The retirement community I am thinking of is like an all-inclusive resort for older persons; almost all of them are retired. It's a leisure-oriented facility with quite a few activities for those who are interested. Like a home away from home sort of situation."

"I see." Elsa bit her lip in thought. Typically, it would have been an easy question to answer, but Mason was watching her keenly as if he expected her to spout nonsense.

"I would do a mini-documentary, outlining the amenities, maybe interview some seniors living there, have the administrators showing the facilities, do some ground shots, highlight some activities. I would place an abbreviated form of this on local television, do some online placements too, targeting that age group, do some radio inserts, but with the budget, I think the bulk of the advertising should be focused on the minidocumentary that can be around for years to come. I could crunch the numbers to see how many radio and television slots I could get on places like cruises, senior citizen associations, and of course, target the about to be retired, see how many brochures I can get into business places…"

She rambled on and on, formulating it as she went along. She was the queen of thinking on her feet, she had to be.

"Thank you, it sounds about what I had in mind and more." Mason cut her off. "The retirement community is real. It is called Golden Acres up in the hills of St. Andrew, eco-friendly, back to nature kind of place. That will be your first assignment."

"So, I am hired?" Elsa was shell shocked. She watched his face in a daze.

"Yes, your job title will be special projects manager, you will report to me directly. I will ask Paxton if he can spare you a marketing assistant, we are a little short-staffed at the moment."

"Special Projects?" Elsa whispered. "Manager as in I head the department?"

"Yes," Mason nodded, "There are times when I need to give special attention to certain advertising jobs, and I am just too busy to do it, or I need help. You will get the bulk of those jobs."

"Tomorrow, when you get here we'll drive up there together, after you report to HR, and you are introduced around. I am afraid there will be no honeymoon period. I have a couple of special projects that I am going to offload on you, if this one works out. It will be the litmus test."

"Got it," Elsa nodded. "You won't regret hiring me."

"I hope not," Mason looked at his watch. "I have to go. I have a function."

"Okay," Elsa said flippantly. "You are calling your dates,

functions now?"

"No," Mason stood up, "It's actually a get together at the Carr's place. I am late."

"They are always having parties." Elsa snorted, "are you going as Yara's date?"

Mason raised an eyebrow. "Would that bother you?"

"No," Elsa got up too and walked toward the door.

A ghost of a smile crossed Mason's face, and she stopped. "You smiled!"

"I smile all the time," Mason said, turning serious again.

"No, you don't. You are not programmed to smile."

"So, you still think I am an android?" Mason chuckled. "I thought you had moved on from that theory when you were fifteen. I think the following year, I was an alien."

"A Vulcan, filled with logic and no emotion," Elsa muttered. "I can't believe you remembered that."

"I remember everything, Elsa." Mason touched the down button for the elevator and turned to look at her. "Every single detail about everything, especially four years ago, when you threw yourself at me. I could have had you then."

Elsa inhaled raggedly and avoided looking at him.

"But I declare a truce," Mason said when they got in the elevator together. "I will not bring up the past, what happened is our secret."

"Agreed." Elsa nodded jerkily.

"It will make working together much easier," Mason said decisively, "if we pretend that we just met."

"Yes," Elsa cleared her throat. "I can do that."

"We probably need to clear the air first though," Mason pressed the stop sign on the elevator and turned to her. "I remember how you look with absolutely, not a stitch on and your expression vulnerable. I remember you begging me to touch you."

Elsa looked at him, her lips trembling. "I got carried away."

"I know," Mason said huskily, "I knew the exact moment you lost the plot. To be honest, I lost it too, and here we are. We have that between us now."

Elsa avoided looking at him. "Well…"

"How many guys have you gotten carried away with since then?"

"I…" Elsa looked away.

"Don't answer." Mason said huskily, "I am not sure I want to know. Through the years, I see your name linked with different men in the papers. Sometimes my mother casually mentions one of your lovers, and I get irrationally jealous."

"You were jealous of me?" Elsa gasped. "You don't even like me!"

"Does it make you feel better to think that?" Mason looked at her solemnly. "Do you think we can work together, Elsa?"

"Yes." Elsa nodded. "I think so."

"We have that incident between us," Mason said huskily. "I am going to need more than an 'I think so' from you."

"I won't show up at your apartment door half-naked and half-drunk. I was an idiot then." Elsa glared at him, "I won't try to test whether you have self-control or not. I will be professional. And for the record, I haven't been with anyone. Sleeping around doesn't appeal to me. You can't believe everything you read."

Mason narrowed his eyes at her. "You begged me to sleep with you."

"Well, I was an idiot at the time. I had been curious about you for many years, you kissed me and touched me before you came to your senses, that is out of the way." Elsa stared in his eyes and then hastily looked away; they felt as if they were pulling her in.

"You wanted to break up my relationship," Mason said

rawly. "You succeeded."

"How did I do that?" Elsa whispered, hyperaware of the tension between them in the confined space of the elevator. "You said you loved her and that what happened between us wouldn't change anything."

"It turns out it changed everything." Mason inhaled raggedly. "You derailed my life that Saturday night. Mission accomplished, Elsa."

He hit the start button, and the elevator started descending.

Elsa's opened her mouth, and no sound came out. "I didn't mean to derail your life. You didn't tell Anna Kay that I was the one who you know…"

"No, I didn't tell her," Mason looked at Elsa broodingly. "If there is even a whiff of sexual overtures in our working relationship, I am firing you," Mason said solemnly when they stepped into the lobby. "I don't want to be tied up in knots over you again. No sexual allurement of any kind. Got it Elsa?"

Elsa nodded mutely.

Chapter Four

Elsa drove home in a daze. Mason said she derailed his life. That made him the best actor in the world because she had not gotten the slightest indication that she had moved him any at all.

He had coldly booted her out of his apartment after she had shown up at his door, and now, he had all but admitted that that little interlude meant something. She grimaced at the thought. It had meant something to her. She had finally kissed Mason Magnus, and he had kissed her back passionately. It had been the best kiss she had ever had, and she had kissed a few men, but none had made her feel like that. She had always known that any kind of intimacy between her and Mason would have been explosive.

It had been short-lived, though. Mason had brought her back down to reality with a bang.

She slowed down in a long line of traffic on Trafalgar Road and wished that she had taken another route.

Usually, at this time of night, there was free-flowing traffic, but there was a party nearby and the traffic had slowed to a crawl. She should have taken a side road. She slumped in her seat, staring at the vehicle in front of her until it was little more than a blur. She indulged herself in one of those memory lane trips that she hated so much.

She didn't like to think too much about the times when she encountered Mason in the past. She forced herself to do so now only because of their encounter tonight and the fact that she would be working with him in the future.

Ten years ago…

"Toddy is getting married again!" Myrna announced it over breakfast one Sunday morning. Toddy wasn't there to tell them himself because he probably slept elsewhere.

Giselle giggled. "Why does he even bother? I thought divorces were expensive."

Tiana was busily typing up some story or the other about herself, and the fictional Wames Walton, who they all knew was her English teacher crush. She was so into it she didn't respond. But for Elsa, the news hit her like a low thud. She made a whimpering sound.

Myrna looked at her sympathetically. "I know you hoped that Toddy would stick around more after he divorced Noreen."

"I did, but it's okay," Elsa said nonchalantly. "Who is he getting married to this time?"

"Celine Magnus," Myrna said disapprovingly. "She lost her husband just three months ago. And already she is marrying Toddy—next Sunday as a matter of fact."

"I have training next weekend," Giselle said. "I can't go."

"I am not going to another of Toddy's weddings." Tiana

looked up from her laptop to add. "Besides, why are we just hearing about this."

"Because they didn't want people to be whispering about the timing," Myrna said. "I must admit I am guilty of that; the timing was the first thing I thought about."

"Where is he going to have it?" Elsa asked dully, "I have nothing better to do next weekend."

"At the Waterfalls. He is keeping it small this time," Myrna muttered. "Maybe because the grieving widow doesn't want the world to know that she is not exactly grieving."

"How many children does this one have?" Giselle asked, "and are they going to be living with us?"

"She has one son. He is twenty-one. Just left college." Myrna shrugged, "I have no idea if he will be living here, but I heard from a very reliable source that he is not interested in this wedding either. The poor boy is still grieving. As his mother should be, I might add."

"But obviously she is not." Elsa pointed out. "I hope she is nice."

"All of Toddy's wives are nice and pretty and professionally accomplished. It's amazing how women like that seem so drawn to him. This one, Celine, I have seen her in the Kingston Chronicles. She looks a little like the singer Sade, and she is a magazine editor." Myrna grimaced. "It's your brother that has issues, not them. He can't stay single for a day."

Elsa usually defended Toddy when Myrna made little jabs at him and his inability to commit to the myriads of women that he had relationships with, but today, she could not. She didn't want to. He was getting married in a week, and he hadn't had the decency to tell them, nor did he introduce them to this latest spouse that he was going to have living with them.

She resented Celine Magnus already, and she hadn't even met her.

"I like Sade." Tiana looked up, "I love the song, No Ordinary Love. I am going to borrow a line for this story, Giana is going to say to Wames, I gave you all the love I got, I gave you all that I can give, I gave you all that I have inside and you took my love…"

Elsa rolled her eyes, "Myrna says she looks like Sade, she's not Sade. Besides, Giana's love for Wames is quite an ordinary everyday love. It will die a horrible death very soon."

"Shut up," Tiana growled. "My love for James will never die. In the future, when I am all grown up, we are going to meet, and we are going to get married."

"Who said anything about you and James?" Elsa chuckled, happy that she had tripped up her sister into admitting that the obviously named Giana and Wames in her story was Tiana and James—she and her high school teacher. It was an impossible story that was never going to happen.

"What magazine is she the editor for?" Giselle mused, in the midst of the bickering.

"Caribbean Styles," Myrna muttered. "I must admit, I like it. I have this month's edition right here."

"Elsa is addicted to it," Giselle grinned. "She's always choosing home designs and drooling over them. She will get on with Celine like a house on fire."

Elsa paused before protesting, Caribbean Styles was her favorite magazine. She and Myrna would pour over its content and drool about the articles. It had beauty trends, travel, style, fashion, interior design, and food topics.

"I don't like her," Elsa growled. "I don't care who she is. I don't want her or her son here!"

"It's not your decision," Giselle said philosophically,

"Toddy can't stay single. He is going to marry someone or move some girlfriend in here shortly. The best we can hope for is that she gets along with Myrna and doesn't upset our routine. I think I am too old for one of Toddy's wives to be acting like a mother. Frankly, I've been getting by just fine."

Elsa nodded. "Of course, we are too old for a mother."

"You are never too old for some mothering," Myrna said. "I am pushing fifty, and my mother still smothers me."

They didn't meet Celine until two weeks later. Toddy had eventually told them about his latest marriage in the same breath he had announced that she would be moving in.

And she had swooped in with a pile of furniture and paintings and reordered the place to look better than it had in years. It looked like something out of one of her magazines.

It didn't take her long to warm up to Celine. She knew how to handle teenage girls without being too overbearing. Celine had also won over Myrna, who could be heard singing her praises day and night.

Celine had carried her own house staff to help Myrna with her workload, and suddenly Myrna had free time.

When Celine was at home and not traveling to some Caribbean locale for her work, she was in the kitchen. Celine loved to cook, and she did it well. She taught Elsa how to make a variety of dishes. She loved to talk and they had their girl chats frequently.

Celine was the best wife Toddy had ever had. She was also the kindest and the most fashion-forward.

The only con, was Celine's son. It took him six months to finally show up to the house.

"He's finishing up uni," Celine would say sadly, "and he is grieving. He was quite close to his dad, but he resents Toddy. He's quite irrational. I don't know how I am going to get him to visit me here."

"You'd like him, Elsa," Celine mused. "Mason is different. He is a good man. A gentleman. I can trust him to do right even when it is not popular. I can't even take credit for the way he is. I think he was born that way. I just had the opportunity to be the one that God blessed to have such an awesome son."

Elsa listened to the glowing descriptions of Celine and thought cynically that it was a mother's love. Nobody was that good.

And then one day, she came home from school, feeling under the weather. Her throat was scratchy, and she was sneezing uncontrollably. Her friend Nadine had told her if she drank a whole gallon of orange juice in one sitting, she would beat the flu. It had worked for her.

And Elsa was on her second glass with her bladder feeling uncomfortably full when Celine walked into the kitchen. As usual, she was dressed impeccably in a red and black work dress with matching shoes. She had her hair pulled back in a sleek bun.

Elsa admired her briefly. She wanted to be like Celine when she grew up. She was effortlessly fashionable and professional, and so pretty.

Celine was probably in her forties, and yet she didn't look it, she didn't have a wrinkle on her mocha toned skin, and her hair was still jet black.

"I have company," Celine said happily. "My baby finally decided to pay his mother a visit."

And in came Celine's baby, a tall, gangly man, wearing a gray shirt and black jeans. He towered over Celine, and he was dark where she was light. He wore super thick glasses and had absurdly pink lips.

Elsa did a double-take. Not because she thought he was particularly handsome but because she was imagining someone who looked a little bit more like Celine. Maybe she had expected a short, light-skinned boy with a babyface. Not a tall, dark, and serious-looking man.

"Elsa, this is my son, Mason."

Mason had stopped at the arch in the kitchen entrance. Celine turned to him. "Come on in, I am going to make your favorite, dinner—roast beef with all of the trimmings. It's Elsa's favorite too."

He was staring at her, and Elsa felt a shaft of discomfort encompass her, the feeling increased when he removed his glasses and blinked. He looked straight at her then, and something inside her shifted.

It felt as if he were pinning her to the spot with his intense stare. His eyes were beautiful. They were dark brown, like deeply polished mahogany. It was a pity they were hidden behind his glasses.

She never forgot that feeling of intensity from that stare.

"Hello Elsa," His voice was husky and deep.

"I am not feeling well." She had choked out. "I am just going to take this orange juice upstairs and try to cure myself."

"That's too bad," Celine said lightly, "I'll come and check on you later."

Elsa had walked quickly out of the kitchen, brushing against Mason, who had reached out a hand to steady her.

That touch had made her feel dizzy, but of course, she had chalked it up to her general feelings of disorientation and the onset of the flu.

*****

She didn't return that first hello, something he had pointed out a year later when he came over to the house and saw her in the sunken living room watching television.

"Hello Elsa," Mason said, sitting across from her.

"Mmph," Elsa responded.

"You know I think you don't have any manners; you have never said hello to me or good evening, good morning, that kind of thing," Mason said conversationally.

Elsa glared at him. "Why do you visit so regularly these days, and why do you always have to say hello to me. I don't mind if you don't."

Mason frowned. "Why are you so hostile? You are like a wild, uncivilized creature."

"And you are always studying me." Elsa rejoined. "That makes you a creepy biologist."

"Biologist?" Mason raised an eyebrow.

"Person who observes and studies the behavior of animals." Elsa grinned. "I am a wild creature you are the creep that creepily watches me so therefore you are a creepy biologist. Don't you have work to do?"

"I run an ad company." Mason murmured. "I like unwinding here. Myrna is pretty good company when my mother is not here."

"Myrna?" Elsa growled. "What about me?"

"You?" Mason snorted. "You are not much of a conversationalist. I check up on you regularly to see if that has changed."

"Do you think I am phat, Mason?"

"You are not fat," Mason said contemplatively.

"I meant pretty, hot, and tempting." Elsa giggled. "Not fat as in big."

"You are pretty but hot and tempting, I don't know about that," Mason said faintly. "I like your sisters, but you are an acquired taste. I am still trying to figure you out. Giselle is a sweet person who is supercharged and hardworking.

She knows what she wants and approaches it with focused precision. She has my kind of dedication. I like that about her. Tiana is a romantic with a genuine spirit, and she is creative and smart. You..."

"What about me?" Elsa asked a tremor in her voice.

"It's like you were raised in the bushes with animals. You grunt and huff like an uncivilized beast, and basic polite gestures seem as if they roll over your head, as for an intelligent conversation, that's an alien concept to you."

"How dare you?" Elsa was livid, "I am civilized and polite!"

"If you didn't look like Giselle so much, I would doubt that you were actually related to the other two girls."

"I hate you!" Elsa squealed.

Mason stared at her unblinkingly. "Are you going to get into a rage now and storm out of the room. Your cartoon is not finished, the pink panther is going to buy a camel."

The cartoon jibe had hit hard. It implied she was young and immature in more than one sense. It wasn't even one of those cartoons with people, it was Pink Panther.

"But you keep seeking me out to hang with. So you do like something about me!" Elsa raged, "You keep coming back for more."

"I have to admit there is something about you that fascinates me. I am not sure what it is." Mason raised an eyebrow. "I still search for meaning."

That was when she stormed out of the room, but Mason's dig had gotten to her. She had no idea why she acted so poorly towards him. Why she was so impolite, why she grunted when he came around.

And so she had vowed to change. Instead of hostility, she tried seduction. She was going to bring Mason Magnus to his knees and make him wish he had called her hot and tempting. She was also going to stop watching cartoons. She found out from his mother that he liked to watch Star Trek and so she got caught up. She had found it pretty boring at first, but the more she watched, the more she got into it.

She then changed her wardrobe. She began to lounge around the house in sexier outfits in the hopes that he would show up and see her.

And when he did show up, Mason greeted her as usual but did not comment on her attire. Nor did he seemed fazed when she started doing her little strip teases from him or bent down to exaggeratingly pick up something or forget to pull up her top when her breasts were exposed.

He discussed Star Trek with her sometimes, his eyes not straying past hers. He was incredibly disciplined and frustrating.

On the day before her sixteenth birthday, she had given him a full striptease down to her brassiere and panties to the song Private Dancer, and Mason had sat through it and then said amusement in his voice, "Elsa, please stick to the books and do something with your life, stripping is not your cup of tea. I haven't been to a strip club, but I think they are more, how should I put this delicately without hurting your feelings, voluptuous is the word. You don't have very much of anything."

She had run away, locked herself in her room, and cried, wishing that she was voluptuous.

That same year, Mason had given Giselle and Tiana expensive handbags on their birthday, and he hadn't given her anything.

It had hurt, but he made himself clear, she had gone way over the line…

Present Day

Elsa snapped out of her reverie when the traffic started moving freely. She had no theories as to why she acted like she did with Mason. Maybe it was because he ignored her. She was never the one of the three sisters to be ignored. She made friends easily. She was the most outgoing of the three. But Mason had blanked her. For most of the year, he made no effort to include her in conversations. He avoided her when he came over to the house. Sometimes she caught him in the kitchen with Myrna having one of their serious conversations. Their heart to hearts as Myrna liked to call it.

"Some woman is going to be so lucky to have him one day," Myrna had said one morning at breakfast. "He is saving himself for someone special. He doesn't want to be a man whore like Toddy."

"What else do you two talk about?" Elsa had asked jealously.

"Stuff," Myrna chortled. "Everything."

"He is too young for you." Elsa had snapped. "You are the same age as Celine!"

Myrna had laughed. "Look who is jealous."

"I am not," Elsa growled. "I don't care!"

But she had been green with it, She had been jealous of Myrna, her dear housekeeper and the only constant mother figure in her life, all because of Mason Magnus.

Elsa grimaced now. Mason had known that she hated rejection and being ignored, and he played her like a fiddle.

It was a puzzle to her why he was the only man that she cared whether or not he ignored her? Whenever she was in Mason's radius, she was reduced to the teenager who craved his attention and wanted to see him lose control.

Four years ago, she had thought she would succeed. She had been overly confident that Mason would take one look at her and lose his mind. She had theorized that she was all grown up, she had grown some boobs, he would wilt at the sight of her in her little red dress.

She would conquer him once and for all, but she had left his apartment humiliated, and she still couldn't shake him out of her mind.

Could she work with him without all of her convoluted thoughts and juvenile emotions stirring her to revert to stupidity?

Chapter Five

Elsa drove up to the townhouse and parked. She alighted from her car so deep in thought that she didn't notice that the lights were on all over the house and the television was blaring.

Tiana was home. She opened the door, and there was her sister curled up in the settee with her favorite low carb ice cream.

"That's my peanut butter fudge ripple!" Elsa said before she even got in the house. "I was saving that for a special occasion."

Tiana laughed. "I didn't like the other flavors. What does pumpkin spice taste like? I wouldn't even try it. I hate anything with pumpkin, it is not my favorite vegetable. And the death by chocolate definitely does not have any sugar, it tastes slightly bitter."

"I ran a campaign for the company." Elsa sat across from Tiana and looked at the ice cream longingly. "They send me new and exciting flavors every month as a thank you."

"This is a ten out of ten." Tiana waved her spoon around. "It's creamy, it's peanut buttery and fudgy."

"I bought that one." Elsa leaned back in the settee. "I could use a tub of it right now, or a drink, definitely a drink."

"I thought you quit drinking because of that mysterious incident that made you change your ways." Tiana grinned. "When you say drink, you mean your zero-carb seltzer water, don't you?"

"Stop making fun of my diet," Elsa muttered. "You'll see when the three of us get older, and I still look young and fresh because of my sugar-free lifestyle. People are going to ask, 'Elsa are those two women with you your grand aunts?'"

Tiana laughed.

"Sugar ages you," Elsa muttered. "You'll see."

"Whatever, man. I am in my twenties. I'll think about aging when I am older." Tiana licked her spoon. "Speaking of looks. Why do you look so fresh after the gym?"

"I was on my way to the gym and was called for a job interview," Elsa sighed, "with Mason Magnus."

"You don't say," Tiana whispered. "Did you get the job?"

"Yup." Elsa nodded. "I am now a special projects manager. I am going to be working with Mason—projects he was asked to personally work on, but because he is too busy pursuing other things, I will handle it or work with him."

"That's awesome!" Tiana rounded her eyes. "Can you manage that?"

"Of course." Elsa fanned her away. "I am looking forward to it, actually. I start working tomorrow."

"Congrats." Tiana chuckled. "You can't tease him now, Elsa. He is your boss.

"I know." Elsa cleared her throat. "He said as much tonight. If I step out of line. I am going to get fired."

"Serves you right." Tiana grunted. "You revert to stupidity when Mason is around."

"I know." Elsa reached for the remote and turned down the television. "I was a little obsessed with getting a reaction from him. It was immature, and I went overboard. I have no explanation as to why he used to rub me the wrong way. I hated him at first sight."

"Are you sure it was hate?" Tiana raised an eyebrow. "You got pretty jealous when he smiled at me or Giselle and didn't smile at you or when he gave us presents and didn't give you one. You even got jealous when he spent time talking to Myrna in the kitchen.

"You used to quiz Myrna about the conversations as if you were a detective! I've said it a thousand times, and you deny it a thousand more. You liked Mason then. It was instant for you, and when he didn't fall at your pretty little feet, you punished him for it."

"Oh, stop it," Elsa said weakly. "I never liked Mason."

"You are still in denial." Tiana shook her head. "You know the difference between the two of us. When I liked James back in high school, I let everybody know. You, on the other hand, kept your liking for Mason a secret and shrouded it into so-called hatred, but you were just as smitten and crazy as I was with James, and Gis was with Pete."

"Shut up," Elsa said tiredly. "None of that is true."

"I say it is." Tiana chuckled. "You claim you were immune from our teenage madness, but you had it bad for Mason. I bet those strong feelings for Mason are still swimming around in your head and your heart. I think he liked you too. You'll never admit it, though, and he probably won't, so you two will never get together. Such a pity. I think you two would be good together. Mason is the right man for you."

"I thought you were a writer, not a pop psychologist. I

am not even going to argue with you," Elsa groaned. "By the way, what are you doing back here. I thought you were staying in St Ann until they start filming?"

"I have to wrap up some things here." Tiana smiled mistily, "like my job."

"You are quitting your job?" Elsa rounded her eyes. "I thought Mr. Oliver grudgingly said you should take all the time you need to make up your mind, why are you burning your bridges?"

"I am not burning bridges." Tiana nodded. "James says the production of the Butlers' Diary will take fourteen to sixteen weeks. I got a job as an assistant director on it. That project will take us into the second week of December. After that, we get married, and I move with him to California."

"Hold up," Elsa held up her hand. "You guys set a date already?"

"Yes, December twenty-sixth, Boxing Day," Tiana nodded. "If all things go according to plan, we want to do an 1800s vintage wedding at the great house at the end of filming. We will have all the things on set for that kind of feel anyway."

"Cool," Elsa nodded. "I could design the invitations for you."

"That would be great, thank you." Tiana nodded. "I will send the invitation list for you by the end of September. I won't be having any bridesmaids or wedding party. James' uncle, Reggie will cater for the event. They do weddings at Morgan Great House all the time. There is even a planner on staff. I'll let her handle the wedding because I'll be working."

Elsa nodded. "Well then, congratulations. Are you happy?"

"Over the moon." Tiana grinned. "I am so happy, I even took Yara's phone call last week."

"How is she?" Elsa smirked. "Is she planning to go after Mason? He went to a function at her parent's place tonight."

"She is fine." Tiana grinned. "See the jealousy showing up again. I don't understand how an otherwise self-aware person can be so blind about her feelings toward a certain male. I should tell Yara to pursue Mason and watch you implode."

"Don't you dare!" Elsa said aggressively. "I am not jealous!"

"Mason is in Yara's top three most desirable men of all time. I think he is a close second behind Ace Jackson. She likes her men tall, dark, and handsome. You should hear her go on and on about having chocolate babies with…"

"And her brother, what's he up to?" Elsa changed the subject. She didn't want to even imagine Mason with another woman and giving her babies. Which was strange considering that she didn't like Mason, and Tiana's theories were crazy.

"Cole is fine." Tiana made a face. "He is seeing someone, and they are talking marriage."

"Say what?" Elsa knocked her ears. "Say that again?"

"No, I won't repeat it," Tiana grinned, "there is nothing wrong with your hearing."

"Who is this woman that Cole Carr is seeing?" Elsa leaned forward.

"Her name is Susan. She's fairly new at church. She sings in the choir; you wouldn't know her because you don't do church."

"Well, well," Elsa sniffed. "It's not as if I don't like church, I think they don't like me. I ask too many questions, and I am too cynical. However, I probably should be going on a regular, you guys have a lot more drama going on than any of my favorite Netflix shows."

Tiana rolled her eyes. "That's not a good reason to go. You are incorrigible."

"No, no, we are not talking about me, don't change the subject." Elsa shook her head. "We are talking about Cole, who swings both ways, and now this girl Susan. Does she know that Cole is ehem…ehem… gay?" Elsa cleared her throat dramatically.

"Yara told her," Tiana said, "and Cole told her too at Yara's insistence, but she doesn't care."

"Really?" Elsa blinked. "Like seriously?"

"Yes," Tiana nodded, "Susan doesn't care."

"Is she hearing impaired? Learning impaired? Anyway impaired?"

"No," Tiana shook her head. "She had always liked Cole, and now he is single. Susan thinks that everybody has something that they struggle with. She will help him in his struggle."

"She's crazy," Elsa muttered. "I think she should not take this on. If she were my girlfriend, I would set her right."

"She probably wouldn't listen," Tiana murmured. "She loves him. Whenever she spoke about him in the past, she would always do it reverently. I realized that she had a crush on him a long time ago. She has the hots for him. I doubt anything that he does or will turn her off. She is all the way turned on."

"And you are okay with this happening?" Elsa widened her eyes. "Yara, is okay with this?"

"My opinion doesn't matter," Tiana shrugged. "I am minding my own business. Yara is probably happy that her brother is moving on, and this time, he is being honest with his potential spouse."

"Someone should have a word with Cole Carr." Elsa snorted. "I think he is making a mistake. He is going to hurt her. How many of those sort of marriages do you see working?"

"I don't know any marriages like that. maybe some of them work, I don't know," Tiana murmured. "It's none of our business what Susan wants to work with. She has the man of her dreams, her eyes are wide open, it's her decision."

"I need to change the subject," Elsa snorted. "It's not my life. I'll mind my own business, as you said. Anyway, Danica will be coming to Jamaica by the end of the week. She wants to live here for a while. I told her that she could stay here since you won't be around."

"Is she on vacation?" Tiana raised an eyebrow. "Wasn't she here in the summer playing detective and looking for our missing grandmother?"

"She quit her job last month and was helping out her parents at their store. I guess when you work for your parents, your vacation days are a bit more flexible."

"Lucky her." Tiana couldn't keep the envy from her voice.

Elsa chuckled. "Now you sound like me before I got my job. Besides, she said she'll be job hunting while she is here. She won't be on vacation".

"I guess I have a touch of envy where Danica is concerned." Tiana mused. "Simply because she had it easy her whole life, and she has both parents who dote on her."

"She is heavily into family too, and as an only child, she is psyched that she has cousins. Cut the girl some slack," Elsa said, "I don't envy her. I just think she is a tad annoying with all of the grandmother stuff. She is obsessed with finding our grandmother. She keeps on texting me about it. She has nobody else to badger with her theories because I was unemployed. Now that I have a job, we are going to have to cool it with our little mystery."

"The Mystery of the Missing Grandmother." Tiana frowned. "Why is she so obsessed about finding her? Obviously, the woman doesn't want to be found, or she is dead. It has been over forty years. How old is Aunt Sara, anyway?"

"Forty-two." Elsa drummed her fingers on the settee. "Which means our granny would be seventy-four now, if she is alive."

"She abandoned her family, Tiana murmured, "that's all there is to it. She left our mother to raise her other children, and she gave up Sara for adoption. She doesn't want to be found. And even if we find her what then? What's the point?"

"Danica just wants to know everything there is to know about her origins. Maybe health wise we can learn something, or I don't know, find out what made her leave her children behind. Elsa shrugged. "Speaking about discovering family, I want to meet Krista Pryce."

Tiana curled her lips. "Giselle and Toddy said as much too. Maybe you guys can invite her to dinner. I heard Caroline will be coming out soon."

"But you'll have to be there," Elsa grinned "and bring the luscious James with you."

"No, thanks." Tiana's phone rang, and she picked it up. "Hi Babe, Elsa, just called your name.

It's James. I am going to take this upstairs." Tiana grinned. "Make sure you remind me about all the family stuff happening so that I can attend, except the Krista one."

"I am not your secretary," Elsa waved her off.

Chapter Six

Mason entered the gardens of the Carr mansion in Upper St Andrew, feeling energized. It didn't take a genius to figure out that his feeling of well-being had a lot to do with him hiring Elsa just a few moments earlier.

He had actually done it. Elsa was in his sphere—working for him. She seemed more mature, and she knew her stuff. He was looking forward to this version of Elsa. He almost felt afraid of what it meant to be working with a mature, levelheaded version of the only woman who had ever appealed to him.

He looked around the brightly lit venue for Cameron, his political fixer, and the only reason he was even at this event.

Cameron dictated where he went and what he did in their war against Toddy Pryce. Some of his suggestions Mason flat out ignored, but tonight he didn't want to ignore this party. Half of the movers and shakers in politics would be around too, and of course, Toddy Pryce himself was there.

He couldn't afford for Toddy to be schmoozing his way through the influential crowd, and he wasn't there to balance it out and do some schmoozing of his own.

That was Toddy's strength; he was the life of the party, a charmer through and through. Mason didn't have what Toddy had naturally, a gregarious personality with the kind of wit and charm to bluster his way through any situation. People naturally liked Toddy, even when he was barreling over them like a freight train. His own mother had been a victim of Toddy Pryce and to see her simpering and genuflecting over Toddy even now was nauseating.

On the other hand, Mason was the opposite of blustery hot air. He was a strategist. He researched and gathered information and watched, content to be in the background before he pounced.

And it was nearing pouncing time. He was going to take down Theodore Pryce soon.

He watched Toddy. As usual, he was the center of attention in whatever group he was in. His hand casually draped around the waist of a beautiful woman, sometimes she would be half his age. His other hand curved around a drinking glass. He would keep that drink in hand all night. He rarely indulged to the point of inebriation. While others slurred their words and gave him information, he would stay sober, gathering information that he could use.

He knew the moment that Toddy saw him. He raised his glass to him and then pulled his date tighter to his side.

Toddy's date, Anna Kay Fuller, was Mason's ex-fiancée. It didn't take a genius to see that Toddy's choice to take Anna Kay to this gathering was no coincidence. The over the top lovey-dovey, touchy-feely, nonsense they were indulging in was supposed to make him jealous.

The only problem with that was he didn't care that Anna

Kay was dating Toddy. His relationship with Anna had ended three years and six months ago, two months before their wedding. Elsa had happened. Well almost happened. He had come to his senses just in time.

"I can't believe Anna is with Toddy," Yara chuckled beside him. "Isn't he like seventy and she like barely in her thirties? What do women see in him? I am looking, but I struggle to see."

"They see power. Women are attracted to power, and he is Toddy Pryce, still handsome and still a charmer." Mason looked at her and smiled. "I think he will lose the 'it' factor when he hits at least ninety or a hundred. At least that's what my mother says, and don't forget she was wife number four."

Yara chuckled. "How is the elegant and lovely Celine?"

"As elegant and lovely as ever." Mason nodded to a passing acquaintance.

"And how are you?" Yara asked. "Found a new fiancée to replace Anna Kay as yet?"

"I wasn't looking." Mason smiled.

"Why did the two of you break up anyway?" Yara asked, "not that I am nosy or anything."

"You are nosy," Mason said to her deadpan.

"Were you to blame?" Yara asked, unperturbed.

"Yes." Mason nodded. "I am not perfect."

"More's the pity. I am still single," Yara grinned, "and I am looking. All my friends are now coupled up. Tiana is getting married in December. It's making me broody. I want a happy ending."

Mason laughed. "But marriage is a happy beginning, not an ending. Relationships take work. Are you ready to put in the work? Knock off some of the selfishness, put somebody's needs before yours."

"Yes, yes, and yes." Yara nodded. "You sure you were the

one to blame? You are so wise."

"Oh yes," Mason nodded, "Anna Kay said I was searching for some way to escape my commitment to her and that I will jeopardize all my future relationships because I am fixated on one particular person."

Yara looked at him unblinkingly. "Who is she?"

"Who is who?" Mason asked innocently.

"The person you are fixated on?"

"I didn't agree with Anna Kay's assessment." Mason shrugged. "Fixated is too strong a word."

"Okay, I'll strike you off my list of eligible bachelors," Yara pouted. "Unless it's me, you are fixated on."

"No, Yara, you are not. Maybe if I had met you before her, who knows?" Mason smiled. "However, you are refreshing to chat to as usual."

"Can anyone join in?" Cameron walked up to them. "I see you two are having an interesting conversation."

"We were talking about what a poor boyfriend I'd make," Mason said ruefully.

"I'd make a good boyfriend," Cameron said, "the harem can attest to it. I have women in my harem with names from A to X. I am currently looking for a Y."

"Not interested." Yara snorted. "My mom is looking for me. If you will excuse me."

She walked away, leaving Cameron shaking his head. "It's because I mentioned the harem isn't it?"

"Maybe, as far as pickup lines go, that was pathetic," Mason said, "I thought you were good at everything."

Cameron laughed. "I am good at finding out everything, there is a difference there."

Mason nodded. "How is our progress with operation find-dirt-on-Toddy?"

"Progressing," Cameron said. "Word on the street is that

he is upset about something, feeling agitated whenever he sees me. That's a tell. Innocent people don't act like that."

"Good." Mason nodded. "That means we are close to something usable."

"Maybe," Cameron shook his head, "or it could mean that he's acting. I have no doubt that Toddy is cooking up a plan to get you to back off. He is not an easy foe, Mason. You might think you are winning, but Toddy has nine lives. You have the business, and the house, that leaves him with seven lives, he'll use them. Be on the lookout for dirty tricks."

"Toddy has skeletons," Mason said. "He has to, find them."

"I will find them," Cameron said uneasily. "The question is, will it be enough to force him to resign."

"It better be," Mason growled. "I want Toddy to not only resign from the senate but to go and lick his wounds in a quiet corner, where I won't have to see and hear from him again."

"Good." Cameron nodded. "I will make that happen. Edmond Greyson is heading this way. I know he is your biggest client; I am going to take my leave."

Mason groaned. Edmond Greyson was the reason he had toned down his bid for revenge against Toddy for years. He had been Toddy's most significant account at Pryceless, and when Mason took over the business and changed the name Greyson was not particularly pleased. He had warned Mason that he had a soft spot for Toddy and Pryceless Advertising. If Mason even put a foot wrong, Greyson would pull all his accounts. And they were large accounts. The billionaire businessman had literally kept Pryceless Advertising afloat. He had business interests in every industry you could think of, and Toddy got most of his marketing budget.

It had been an uneasy four years with the Greyson breathing down his neck, watching him like a hawk.

He turned and smiled at Edmond. It had to be a genuine smile. Edmond could spot fakery a mile away, and he usually called out people on it.

He was a stocky light-skinned man with a huge belly, grey sideburns, pug nose, gray eyes that were a bit too close together, and a high forehead. Legend had it that his father was a wealthy tourist, and his mother was a housekeeper at the villa where he had stayed during a visit to Jamaica. The father had left the island without knowing that his mother was pregnant, and Greyson had grown up rough. He made his first million before he was twenty-five after renovating an old house his maternal grandmother had given him and turning it into a hotel. He had branched out into many other industries since. They called him Midas Greyson in the business world.

"Mason Magnus," Edmond shook his hand. "How are you?"

"I am doing good." Mason smiled. "I don't have to ask how you are. I read in the paper last week that you acquired a chocolate company."

Edmond chuckled. "The wife wanted it. So I got it for her birthday."

Mason nodded. "Happy wife, happy life. How is Mrs. Greyson?"

"Heather is great." Edmond squinted at him. "She likes you, you know that? Calls you an exemplary young man."

"Yes." Mason nodded. "She has said so many times in my hearing. I try to live up to it."

"It has come to her attention that Elsa Pryce is out of a job."

"Not anymore," Mason looked at his client, puzzled. "I hired her just tonight. I didn't know you were interested in Elsa?"

"My wife is interested in Elsa," Edmond Greyson laughed. "She has a fascination with the triplets as she calls Toddy's sisters. They are her favorite orphans. She will be pleased to hear you hired Elsa. It's a good move for you, consider your company shortlisted for the chocolate company account, Edmond Junior is running this one. Come with your best pitch in three weeks."

Greyson moved on after that, and Mason stared after him puzzled. Why was Heather Greyson interested in Elsa?

He didn't have much time to ponder the question in depth when Toddy Pryce walked by him and then stopped.

"Mason," Toddy said cordially.

"Toddy," Mason answered in kind.

"I heard you hired my sister," Toddy said. "Thank you. Somebody blackballed her all over town. I know we have our difference, and you didn't have to do it."

"Elsa is an asset. It wasn't a hard decision to make."

Toddy smiled. "You always had a soft spot for her, didn't you?"

Mason narrowed his eyes at Toddy. "What is that supposed to mean?"

"Nothing." Toddy held up his hand. "It's a totally innocent observation based on stuff I've heard from Myrna and your mother. We don't have to be in mortal combat all the time, you know."

"I don't trust anything you say." Mason growled. "Everything is calculated and has a hidden meaning."

Toddy sighed. "I wish you wouldn't be so distrustful. Your father and I were good friends."

Mason snorted. "I don't think so."

"We were a team in the early days." Toddy sighed. "I wish you had a different understanding of what went on in the past. Maybe you wouldn't be so angry all the time."

"So enlighten me," Mason growled. "Tell me about this past, of unity and love with my father. And then explain to me why you wanted everything he had, even my own mother…"

"I wish you weren't so angry," Toddy said soothingly. "It would make life easier for everyone."

Mason gritted his teeth. "I have no intention of making life easier for you Mr. Pryce. I am going to make you pay for everything you have done to my father."

Toddy shook his head and looked at him sorrowfully. "An eye for an eye leaves everybody blind."

It was this parting shot before he was whisked away to some other conversation that robbed Mason of a retort.

Chapter Seven

Elsa dressed carefully the next day before heading into work. She didn't want to be accused of being provocative. She had seen the determination in Mason's eyes when he had warned her not to make any sexual overtures. Not that she would have made any. He was a bit presumptuous, wasn't he?

She put on her basic black pants suit, a red under blouse, and a slash of bright red lipstick. She brushed down her curls until they were sculpted to her head and put two regular nobs in her ears. There was nothing provocative about how she looked. Tiana widened her eyes when she breezed pass to the front door.

"Wow," Tiana grinned. "So this is you dressing asexual? Unsexy?"

"Yes," Elsa looked at herself in the hallway mirror. "What's wrong?"

"You are the fairest of them all," Tiana said sarcastically.

"A real showstopper. Mason won't be able to concentrate. Your lips are too shiny and crimson. They shout come hither, Mason."

Elsa frowned at her reflection. "So, I should lose the red lippy?"

"Yup." Tiana nodded. "Or at least lose some of the sheen."

"Okay." Elsa snapped, rummaging in her bag for a wet wipe.

Tiana giggled. "You are going to work with Mason Magnus. I can't believe this."

"Maybe this will be my first and last day." Elsa opened the door. "We'll see."

"I doubt it will be your last. Mason is not going to let you go ever again." Tiana grinned. "If he has any sense at all, he'll work on letting you see what has been obvious to everyone these past couple of years."

"What's obvious?" Elsa turned to Tiana reluctantly.

"That your animosity toward him is manufactured, thrown up to defend and protect your fragile heart."

"Stop the psychobabble," Elsa growled. "And stop putting ideas in my head. I know when I like someone. I never liked Mason Magnus."

Except for that weekend four years ago, when she had not only liked him, she had handed him herself on a platter and was soundly rejected. She would never dare say that part out loud.

Tiana grinned. "So why do you still wear that necklace he bought you for your sixteenth birthday?"

Elsa adjusted her necklace self-consciously, though it wasn't visible under her clothes. "It means nothing."

"Keep telling yourself that," Tiana grunted. "You look good, by the way. Really nice."

"Thank you." Elsa smiled. "Your stupid theories aside, I

am going to miss you when you go to St Ann, and then you'll be married and moving away. I will not ruin my mascara by crying over the likes of you."

Tiana grinned. "I will be here until tomorrow, and Gis is coming over tonight. We can have a rare girl's night."

"Good." Elsa blinked away the weak tears that were threatening. All of a sudden, it hit her that moments like this with Tiana would end very soon. She didn't expect to feel so vulnerable about it.

"See you later." She blew Tiana a kiss and stepped out.

****

The drive up to the hills was mostly done in silence. After asking her what she thought about the HR tour and her new office, which was beside his, Mason had gone silent.

Elsa was not comfortable with long stretches of unbreakable silence. It made her want to twitch.

"Do you want the radio on?" Mason asked after a while.

"Yes, thank you," Elsa said in relief.

"You can't be quiet with your own thoughts, can you?" Mason chuckled. "You are like a fish out of water when you are not performing."

"Performing?" Elsa looked at him fiercely.

"All of life is a stage, and you are an active player, not a wallpaper," Mason glanced at her, "a wallpaper like me."

"I said that when I was fifteen. I was trying to get a rise out of you at the time. You were so self-contained and aloof." Elsa muttered. "For someone who wants to pretend that we are just meeting, you surely remember a lot of the things that I said and did back when I was a bratty teenager."

He didn't respond, and Elsa glanced at him out of the corner of her eye. He was staring straight ahead.

He felt her stare and looked at her and then sighed. "You are right, I apologize."

"It's fine, it is a lapse, first-day kinks. It's hard to pretend that you don't know someone when you actually do. I should be the one apologizing. I really am sorry for my behavior in the past. I must have hurt you with the things I said and… did. Plus, there was four years ago…"

"You didn't hurt me. That is not the emotion that readily comes to mind when it comes to you." Mason shrugged. "You are absolved of your perceived sins against me, Elsa."

What are the emotions that readily come to mind when you think about me? Elsa wanted to ask. She bit her lip, squeezing back the question.

She didn't want to hear the answer if it was not complimentary. She was feeling a little vulnerable where Mason was concerned, and she blamed Tiana for putting thoughts in her head. Her sister didn't know squat about her feelings toward Mason. The first time she saw him, it had been instant dislike. And the feeling had been mutual, except that she had noticed his cologne then. She had inhaled deeply when he had stepped into the room, and that scent remained her favorite to this day.

She looked out at the passing scenery, trying to dispel the thought.

He smelled good this morning as he did all the time, and he appeared as devastatingly handsome as he had looked last night. Today he was dressed a little more formally in white shirt and black pants.

He looked the part of a high-powered marketing executive without his full battle armor on. Mason had always screamed serious business.

She turned on his CD player, curious to see what he was listening to.

Dennis Brown's song came on, If I had the world. I would give it to you...

"You like Dennis Brown, huh?" Elsa chuckled, "just like Toddy. The two of you have more in common than I thought."

"Oh, really?" Mason growled. "What do I have in common with your brother?"

"Everything." Elsa chuckled, "you are in advertising, he was in advertising, you even bought his former home, you must have loved the architecture."

"It was my home before his," Mason growled. "I just repurchased it. As for being in advertising, it was half my father's company before Toddy took it over and renamed it. Too bad, he blithely forgot that fifty percent of the shares belonged to a Magnus. I am my father's heir. I just took back my shares when I could and bought his. Toddy is a destroyer."

"Toddy is a savior," Elsa countered, "and he is a very good family man. I can understand the house and the business, but why are you trying to take over his Senate seat! Why are you so obsessed with him?

"I am not obsessed with him," Mason sighed. "He schmoozed his way into the senate seat my father held. He was all over the Prime Minister before my father was even buried. And he charmed his way into my mother's life, they got married three months after my father died.

"It was so quick; people were speculating that they were together while she was married to my dad."

"Were they?" Elsa asked.

"My mother says no." Mason tapped the staring wheel uncomfortably.

"But you don't believe her, do you?" Elsa whispered. "And that is a part of your anger."

Mason looked at her in surprise. "How did you deduce

that?"

"Well, there is Toddy's reputation with women, and the fact that your father was so busy it actually killed him. I think that all wasn't as rosy in your parent's marriage."

"I don't know." Mason shrugged. "I am an only child; I thought my family was perfect. My parents didn't act like they had any issues. Yes, my dad was rarely home, but when he was there, we spent quality time together."

"I don't think you should be mad at Toddy about your mother." Elsa mused.

"Why shouldn't I be, he cheated on her with his secretary in their marital bed. He broke my mother and for a good while she stayed broken. You know how she was full of life and laughter. It's like Toddy squeezed all of it out of her and I had to watch it happen."

"And maybe it was karma for her," Elsa said out loud.

"Karma?" Mason raised an eyebrow. "That sounds so mean coming from you. I thought you liked my mom. You two seem to get on like a house on fire."

"I do like Celine," Elsa protested, "but she knew who she was marrying. She knew she was the fourth wife. I don't know what really went down before your father died, but knowing Toddy, you should be asking your mother some serious questions about when her relationship with him started, and if she was fooling around with a man who couldn't be faithful if you paid him."

"You have a point," Mason grunted. "I thought my mother grieved more about Toddy cheating on her than she did about my father's death. She certainly spent a long time in mourning after her marriage to Toddy ended. I couldn't understand it."

Elsa cleared her throat. "She loved Toddy. She said it over and over again."

"I know." Mason sighed, "that much is obvious. I think even now if he said he wanted them to get married again, she would jump at the chance. It makes me sad that she didn't love my dad like that."

"So your obsession with Toddy and this vendetta against him is some kind of misguided justice for your father?" Elsa asked. If only Tiana could see her now, using her psychobabble. She even sounded like her sister while asking the question.

Mason glanced at her contemplatively. "I am not obsessed with Toddy, au contraire, I think Toddy was the one obsessed with everything that belonged to my father. Ask him why he coveted everything that belonged to Manuel Magnus. If he gives you an acceptable answer I will back off."

Elsa sighed. "You are just saying that. If I confront Toddy about this and he gives me an acceptable answer about why all of this happened, you are saying you will back off?"

"I did say if it was an acceptable answer." Mason pointed out. "I am not an unreasonable man, but Toddy declared war against my father, whether he knows it or not. As my father's son, I will fight for his legacy, and I will not give up until Theodore Pryce is defeated."

"Or dead." Elsa glared at him. "You are stressing out my beloved brother until he has a heart attack and dies."

"I wouldn't go as far as to say that." Mason mused, "but I can't say the thought hasn't crossed my mind, after all, Toddy did have a hand in pushing my father to a heart attack."

"That's absurd," Elsa gasped. "Nothing good ever comes from revenge, and you are fighting in a war that you don't fully understand."

"What makes you say that?" Mason asked.

"You need to know their story. You need to know the why of things, get the background between your father and Toddy.

You need to understand."

"I understand it, I lived it," Mason said stubbornly. "And I don't want Toddy's biased perspective about anything. He wouldn't tell me the truth."

"You have more passion for this than anything I have ever seen," Elsa said in awe.

"When I am focused on something I go all in," Mason looked at her briefly and significantly then back at the road, and Elsa felt her heartbeat skyrocketing.

He was referring to four years ago. Her first introduction into what it meant when Mason went all in. Her first glimpse into a passionate Mason.

"So how do you know Ace Jackson?" Elsa asked, changing the subject quickly, not wanting to think about four years ago.

"He is my cousin. His mother, Celia, is my mother's aunt. They are really close. We used to visit them in Portland when Ace Senior had a practice there, and we pretty much are always at each other's family gatherings."

"Yes, I know about that story." Elsa chuckled. "Did you know that my cousin Guy and Ace were in competition over a girl back there when Ace went to sort out his father's practice and the family house?"

"Yes," Mason grimaced. "Ace was heartbroken for a while, but he attended their wedding.

"I know, I saw him," Elsa murmured. "He spent most of the time by himself. I watched him and thought to myself, why is he putting himself through such torture."

"He wanted to show that he was strong and that there were no hard feelings." Mason murmured. "I don't think I would have attended myself. I am no stickler for punishment. If the girl I loved was getting married to someone else, best believe I would be in a far corner somewhere licking my wounds."

"Plotting how you were going to break them up? Or how you would stop the wedding?" Elsa grinned. "I would be doing just that. See, we have something in common."

"If we talk long enough, we will find that there are some points at which we intersect." Mason said cheekily. "We are both human beings after all."

Elsa glared at him. "You are not going to let me forget that I thought you weren't human, are you?"

Mason chuckled.

Elsa stared at him in awe.

He laughed even louder. "I won't let you forget it if you keep acting astonished when I laugh."

"It's just that," Elsa swallowed, "I have never seen you so…"

"Relaxed, not wound up. It's this place, they started ascending the hill, I love it here in the Gordon town Hills. Quade Jackson has a place near here. He even has a stream in the backyard."

"Tell me about Quade Jackson." Elsa frowned. "I never heard about him before."

"He was the only child for Jacob Jackson, Ace Jackson Senior's brother." Mason shrugged. "His parents died in a car accident when he was a young boy. His granduncle, Tobias Jackson raised him, right here in these hills."

"Oh," Elsa widened her eyes. "And Tobias was the one who owned Golden Acres?"

"Correct." Mason nodded. "He left the majority of shares in Golden Acres to Quade and Ace Junior. They were the only grandnephews who showed any interest in the place, and he wanted it to be in good hands."

"And they do take it seriously. They upgraded Golden Acres in the past two years and turned it into quite the resort-style place, and they want everyone to know about it. That's where we come in."

"Is Quade a doctor too?" Elsa asked.

"No, a businessman." Mason grimaced, "and one of my oldest friends. He knows a lot about you. I bet he'll be shocked to see us together."

"You talked to him about me?" Elsa glared at Mason. "What did you tell him?"

"He knows how you drove me crazy." Mason murmured. "I may have vented my frustrations about you to him before."

Elsa smiled.

"It is nothing to smile about," Mason muttered. "You have no idea what you did to me when you showed up at my doorstep four years ago, and we are not going to discuss it."

"Fine," Elsa muttered, "but I think you want to talk about it. I think you like to think about the things I used to do."

Mason glanced at her but didn't answer. He turned into a flower-lined driveway flanked with yellow allamanda and hibiscus flowers. There was a wooden sign at the front with gold lettering that said, Golden Acres. It already had a resort feel. That was confirmed when Mason parked before a building that said reception and office.

"I would live here," Elsa chuckled, "and I am not retired."

"They do have job openings. Mason glanced at his watch, "and there is staff accommodation."

"You don't say," Elsa mused, "like what positions?"

"I remember Quade mentioning that they need a recreation director. Their beloved recreation director is leaving. The residents here liked her. Quade was bemoaning the fact that whoever replaced her had big shoes to fill."

"Mmm." Elsa mused.

"You just started working for me," Mason said in warning. "I hope you are not thinking of quitting now."

"No," Elsa mused. "I was thinking of my cousin Danica.

She will be staying with me for a while. This job might be right up her alley. I am going to tell her about it."

Mason shrugged. "Once you are not planning to bail on me, I am fine with it. Put your game face on. We are about to get busy."

Chapter Eight

The place was lovely. Someone had deliberately planted only yellow blooming trees and shrubs and flowers all over the property playing on the Golden theme. Even the poui tree in front of the offices was in full yellow bloom.

She walked up the brick pathway behind Mason and smiled to herself. This was going to be an easy sell. It was a gorgeous location with an unparalleled view of the city in the distance.

A tall thin guy came to greet them at the reception desk. He introduced himself as Devin, Quade's assistant.

He kept glancing at her every chance he got. Elsa grinned. Mason looked at her and shook his head.

"And so it begins," he said under his breath. "The Elsa effect."

Elsa grinned even wider.

Devin led them to the conference room, where Ace was standing in a corner talking on the phone. Quade, she assumed, was studying a document, and a middle-aged lady with a tapered cut hairstyle was on a computer.

"Hey," Quade looked up when they entered the room and then got up energetically. He was a handsome guy—the same height as Mason. He was leanly muscular, medium brown complexion, cleanly shaven, and had hazel eyes.

He didn't look much like his cousin, Ace, who was tall, dark, and classically handsome.

"Hello Mason and Elsa," Quade shook their hands and smiled at her warmly. Elsa, it's nice to finally meet you."

She nodded awkwardly. She wondered what Mason had confided to him about her. It probably wasn't anything too bad because Quade's smile didn't slip. He seemed like he was genuinely pleased to meet her. He introduced them to the lady who was busy typing, her hands flying over the keys of the keyboard.

"This is Lily Pikeman, the administrator here."

Lily stopped typing long enough to acknowledge them and shake hands. They exchanged pleasantries waiting for Ace to finish his phone call.

Elsa looked around the spacious conference room, and her eyes met Quade's who had been studying her with unabashed curiosity.

"I am sorry for staring," Quade said without any apology in his voice, "but you look so much like Giselle. Somehow, I didn't expect you to look so much like her. Mason always said it was easy to tell you three apart. He always said he could pick you out of a crowd quite easily."

Elsa turned to Mason. Is that so?

Mason barely blinked. "Tell us about Golden Acres, Quade. Elsa and I are pretending that we just met."

"Oh, role-playing, how exciting." Quade grinned when Mason glared at him.

"Well, the basics. Golden Acres was founded by my grand uncle Dr. Tobias Jackson. He specialized in geriatric medicine in the States, and he worked at a lush retirement community in Florida. He decided to replicate the concept here.

"He had the vision of a luxurious retirement community with all the amenities of an all-inclusive hotel. A perpetual vacation where seniors can live and have hobbies and activities to keep them occupied so that they don't feel lonely. We are like a cruise ship but always docked."

Elsa nodded. "It is a lovely concept."

"He started with ten two-bedroom bungalows, two restaurants, a concierge, and a smorgasbord of activities that will boggle the mind. Pretty soon, the bungalows were not enough, and he expanded. We now house fifty permanent residents. Some of the residents still work, a few of them are semi-retired. Our biggest clientele, however, are the seasonal residents. Some of them stay for six months out of the year and others for three or four. We are a luxury home away from home business.

"We have seen an uptick in demand for short term residents, mainly from Europe. Some months we are overbooked, so two years ago, we had to turn away winter bookings from our short-term clients. It broke our hearts.

"That's why Ace and I decided to expand the operation. Keeping the luxury concept, we built accommodation catering for one hundred short term guests, and that's where you come in. We need Magnus Communication to fill up the place for us."

Ace got off the phone. "Sorry about that, folks. I had a whale of a time convincing my patient to take her medication. Elsa, I haven't seen you in ages, you look gorgeous as usual."

Elsa smiled. "Thank you, you are looking gorg yourself!"

Mason scowled. "Enough of the mutual admiration, let's get on with it."

Ace guffawed. "And it's great to see you too, cousin."

"Sure it is," Mason grunted.

"Ace will give you two a tour while I have a little personnel meeting with Lily, we are short-staffed at the moment." Quade grimaced. "Our precious Amelia will be leaving, some of the residents are emotionally attached to her."

"That's your recreation director?" Elsa asked.

"Yes," Quade nodded. "If you know of anyone who has a warm personality, who is really good with older people and wouldn't mind living up here on the weekdays. You can email me his or her résumé."

Elsa nodded.

Ace headed to the door, and Elsa followed.

Mason's phone rang. He looked at the screen. "I have to take this; I'll catch up with you two in a bit."

****

"How old do I have to be to live here?" Elsa asked, turning to Ace after inspecting one of the rooms. They were standing in one of the newer bungalows which was not yet occupied. They had the best views.

Ace chuckled. "I doubt you'd like it here, Elsa, it's not up to your speed. Most of our residents appreciate a quieter life. You would go bonkers."

"I wouldn't mind it; I like older people." Elsa grinned. "And they like me. My brother is passed retirement age, and I am his favorite sister. He says I keep him young and entertained."

"Does he know that you are working for Mason?" Ace asked.

"I haven't gotten around to telling him yet." Elsa shrugged. "I try not to mention Toddy when I am around Mason, and I try not to mention Mason when I am around Toddy. I know there is tension there."

"Tension is putting it mildly." Ace lead the way out of the cottage. "I have known Mason since we were kids, and the period between his father dying and his mother marrying Toddy were pretty dark days for him. It shook him up pretty badly and changed him."

"I know." Elsa sighed. "I was around, I kind of added to the darkness."

"I doubt that," Ace grinned. "I think you may have toned it down. When he met you, he went from dark suffocating grief with the world on his shoulder to hopeful man with a purpose."

Elsa frowned. "I wasn't nice to Mason when I was younger. He was so silent and watchful, and I couldn't stand it. I may have been a tad too over the top with him."

Ace chuckled. "At least you made him feel something else other than despair."

"That's so true," Elsa chuckled. "You should hear when we used to trade barbs at each other. I called him names, and then he would call me names. Mason was never good for my ego."

"Not everyone writes poems and gives gifts," Ace said. "Maybe trading insults was his way of getting your attention. You never forgot him, did you? In a world of adoring men, he stood out."

"Adoring men." Elsa widened her eyes. "I don't live in that world."

"Oh, you do," Ace winked at her. "You are exceptionally pretty, and if pursuing you wouldn't bring the wrath of Mason on my back, I probably would join the adoring public."

"Thank you for the compliment, Ace, but there is no breaking Mason's heart because we are not ever going to be in that sort of situation." Elsa frowned. "One, he is my boss, and two, he is Mason. He doesn't like me much, and I don't like him."

Her voice petered away when she said that. It didn't have the kind of conviction that would convince anyone, especially someone as smart as Ace.

Ace laughed dryly and changed the subject. "Now that you have seen the infrastructure, you need to see some of the activities that our residents participate in."

"I know there is hiking," Elsa pointed to a hiking trail that disappeared into the evergreen trees lining a mountainside.

"And hobby groups," Ace said and classes. "Some of the retirees here teach classes and help others with various hobbies. One of the most popular courses is our creative writing class. That one is conducted by my aunt Florence, Tobias' widow.

"Creative writing?" Elsa whispered. "I hope I don't have to listen to any of the stories. I don't have the time."

"You will get volunteers bombarding you with stories," Ace said. "We'll let them down easy."

They followed the path to a building with a sign that said, 'The Hobby House'. It was mostly glass on the outside and was surrounded by black-eyed Susans. The yellow blooms were so prolific, they wound their way down the slope.

"Wow," Elsa whispered. "It's like a yellow sea. If I am going to do an infomercial, I need to get an aerial shot of this."

They walked into the hobby building a sprawling area with partitions. Various classes were going on. Some of them had a few people, the creative writing class had about ten seniors. The teacher, Ace's Aunt Florence, was a petite woman of indiscriminate age. Her face was barely lined, her wavy hair was dyed a very vivid lavender and cut in the same style as Elsa had hers, short at the sides, more on the top. And she was dressed in a caftan swirling with various colors of purple.

She flitted from one end of the class to the other, full of energy and excitement.

She was too energetic for her class—half of them were asleep, but it didn't seem to faze her.

"Okay, class, I am going to share a story." She said just as Ace and Elsa walked in.

Elsa smiled. "That is how I am going to look when I am that age. I will be a sexy granny, full of vim, vigor, and vitality."

Ace laughed out loud, and most of the class looked back at him. A few of them were still sleeping.

Florence looked across at them and smiled. "My grandnephew Ace and…"

"Elsa Pryce, from Magnus Communications," Elsa cleared her throat. "Sorry to crash your class."

"I don't mind." Florence smiled. "You two have a seat, you are just in time to hear the story."

Elsa looked at Ace wearily.

"It's not long," Florence hurried to reassure her. "Are you Ace's new lady?"

"No," Elsa smiled.

"Why ever not?" One of the old ladies at the front asked. She had a bundle of knitting in her lap and what looked like a pattern book beside it. "Dr. Ace is scrumptious. He has the perfect bedside manner. Maybe he has a good in bed manner too, I proposition him now and again, but he always says no, but maybe that's because mature women are not to his taste."

A few of them laughed.

"Now Dorothy," Florence turned to the lady with the

knitting, "didn't we decide not to interfere in Dr. Ace's love life."

Dorothy shrugged. "But it's my favorite hobby because he is my favorite doctor."

Ace chuckled. "I am flattered, Dorothy, but Elsa is here to work. You will see her around for the next couple of weeks."

"You work with Mason Magnus?" Dorothy grinned, showing her dentures. "Is Mason here? I need to see him. I want to advertise my blankets. She held up the misshapen thing she was knitting. And only because of that, I have no outright designs on Mr. Magnus. He is handsome but a bit too serious for my taste."

Elsa chuckled.

"Are you single, dear?" Dorothy asked, delighted that Elsa had engaged her.

"Yes," Elsa nodded.

"Dr. Ace is single," Dorothy grinned, "and Mr. Mason is single too. "Though why either of them are in that state is beyond me. Something must be wrong with the women in their sphere. Don't you think so, dear?"

"Shut it, Dorothy," Florence smiled. "It's time for the story."

She clapped her hands twice and the sleeping few woke up.

"Now we are all going to listen. It is an excerpt from my book, Notes About My Life."

Elsa stifled a groan. She sat down with Ace at the back of the class and prepared herself to be bored, people always thought that their lives were more interesting than it really was, and they just had to share it with the world.

Florence started reading.

His big bulk snuffed out the light of the hallway behind him. I cowered in the bed, pulling my legs into a fetal-like position. He grunted as he leaned on the doorjamb sticking his hands into his pockets. I clutched the threadbare sheet that smelled like the lime tree it had been thrown on earlier in the day to dry.

He stepped closer to the bed. The walls of the room seemed as if they had shrunken with his approach, its unpainted cement splattered surface seemed even more menacing than he was. I hated these walls. They absorbed the sounds of my screams, and they stood silently by as I got hurt. They never told anyone about what they saw, but when he approached, they drew nearer, eager to see my defilement.

I looked around the cramped space of the room wildly, the chair that I had put at the door earlier to halt his entry laid on its side in an undignified sprawl. Beside the chair was a torn plastic bag with my clothes. My school uniform hung out of the gash like a dead fish spilling its guts. My only other possession was a drawing I had made of my family. It clung to the wall on one piece of tape.

I had drawn my mother. She was standing on the step of our four-room dwelling. She looked tired and careworn. She worked at the hospital in the days as a janitor and went to school in the evenings.

Beside my mother was my older sister, Ivy, who was fourteen years old. Her hand resting on the bulk that was her belly, her finger stuck in her mouth, a look of bewilderment on her face. She was sent to our grandmother's house to have her child; she could not have the baby in our district. People were talking, they were saying that Ivy's pregnancy was a mystery; they were asking who was the father of her child.

My father was noticeably absent from the picture on the wall. He never seemed to notice my picture or his absence from it when he came to my room at night. I could hear his heavy breathing as he advanced into the room. I smelled his overheated body; he carried the pungent odor of the cows he took care of on the dairy farm where he worked.

My foot touched the knife that I had secretly brought to my room after dinner. It nicked me, and I grimaced with pain. I could feel the blood slowly trickling on the sheet. I fervently hoped he couldn't see the outline of the knife or the bright red spot of blood that was slowly seeping through the thinness of the sheet. He put a leg on the bed and reached for my trembling body.

Then the clock struck nine somewhere in the house. The faint sound of its chiming seemed to stop his progression onto the bed. He looked at his watch, his beefy hair roughened arm raised impatiently. He squinted to read it in the limited light.

"This is always wrong," he mumbled crossly.

I held my breath; nine o'clock meant that it was time for Mommy to get home. Nine o'clock meant that I would not be hurt. Nine o'clock meant that I had one more night's reprieve from him and his foul breath fanning my face, his burly girth pinning me to the bed.

I shuddered in the silence of his retreat and hid the knife under the bed for another night.

"Wow," Elsa muttered. "That's fascinating stuff."

"I agree," Ace murmured. "Aunt Florence is certainly brave to be hanging it all out to dry. You know she is a relative by marriage because my blood family are as tight-lipped as they come about our family issues."

Florence came to meet them from the front of the class. "How was it?"

"I wish I could hear more. Like what eventually happened to you and your sister. Your childhood was dismal."

"It was, but my mother and I escaped." Florence giggled

girlishly. "If you come back next week, there will be another installment."

"I'll be here," Elsa said.

"Good," Florence smiled.

"I am sorry we have to break this up," Ace said, glancing at his watch, "but we have to continue with the tour. "We still have to check out the spa and the gym."

"Okay, go on," Florence smiled. "I guess I will see you around, Elsa. When you get here come and find me, we can have a chat over tea."

"I will do just that." Elsa smiled. "There was something about Florence that felt familiar. Maybe it was the shape of her face. Maybe it was the way that she smiled. It reminded her a bit of her aunt, Sharla. Maybe that was how Sharla would look when she is Florence's age."

She followed Ace to another building where there was an elaborate spa, a gym with a handsome, chunky instructor putting some ladies through the paces in the weight room.

"That's Lee Wiley, he runs the gym." Ace waved to Lee, who was spot-checking an enviable looking older woman with muscles that made Elsa's look puny.

"Wiley?" Elsa raised an eyebrow.

"Micky Wiley's cousin's son or something like that." Ace frowned. "Lee is from the Valleys. Micky asked me to hire him, it was a good choice."

"He looks so much like you," Elsa whispered. "The same eyes and height if you bulked up like him somebody could mistake you two for brothers."

Ace glanced at her sharply. "I don't see it."

Elsa cleared her throat. "You haven't sorted that out yet, have you?"

"Sorted what out?" Ace asked innocently.

"The reason why you look so Wileyesque." Elsa cleared

her throat. "You have the same hooded eyes. All the Wileys seem to have it. The same nose too."

Elsa inspected him feature by feature. "Yup, the eyes are a dead giveaway. My aunt Sharla calls it bedroom eyes."

"But I am a Jackson," Ace said easily. "The eyes are just a coincidence."

"I would want to know my true origins." Elsa snorted. "The coincidence in looks to the Wileys is just too uncanny."

"It's just a coincidence," Ace said stubbornly. "I have family dynamics to think about. I am the junior to my father's senior, and I don't want to upset the way things are. I don't want to talk about this again."

"Fine," Elsa nodded, "but what if you fall in love with your own sister?"

"If we are assuming that I am a Wiley, Micky doesn't have any children, so there is no chance of that." Ace said, exasperation creeping in his voice.

"He may though," Elsa pointed out grimly. "He may have fathered a dozen or more of you, and they were given to different fathers. You could one day date your sister! You have to at least find out if that could be a possibility."

Ace looked upset. He turned away from her slightly, and Elsa felt a pang of regret for saying it. It wasn't professional, and it was none of her business.

She was so happy when Lee finished spot-checking his client and came over to them. She would have melted in mortification otherwise.

"You must tell me if you want shots of the gym empty or with my classes going," he grinned. "Our morning classes are usually super packed. We even have swimming exercises for the wheelchair-bound."

"Thanks, I will let you know." Elsa nodded.

Lee saluted and went back to his client.

"So, what do you think?" Ace asked when they were on the path heading back to the offices.

"The place is great. The aesthetics, the amenities, it won't be a hard sell at all. My only concern is that you will be overbooked when I am done."

She paused. "I am sorry, Ace, about earlier. I should have kept my big mouth shut."

Ace shook his head. "Don't worry about it. It's not as if those things haven't crossed my mind either. I should clear up the speculation about my parentage once and for all."

"Why haven't you?" Elsa frowned. "You are a doctor, you have access to Micky Wiley, get a swab from him, and test it. And then you'll find out if you are a Wiley or not. You won't have to tell a soul what you learn."

"My mother asked me not to, even though I wanted to find out a couple years ago." Ace shrugged. "But my mother says if I go through with this testing, I would be essentially calling her a liar and a cheater. Ace Jackson Senior is my father, she never slept with Micky Wiley, the gardener, and all of this speculation is hurtful to her."

"Micky told Guy he was your father," Elsa said. "I guess it boils down to who you believe.

"Micky is known to have one too many drinks," Ace said. "He could have been living out his fantasies. My mother was a lonely housewife, and he was her gardener. He probably saw the situation and spun some fantasies."

"Well, there is that." Elsa mused. "I know how Micky gets when he's drunk. I just never thought of him as a fantasy spinner. Well then, I am sorry for the unprofessional speculation. On to other members of your family, your aunt Florence…that story was incredible. Obviously, she came out of that situation, and it was many years ago, but still..."

"Yes," Ace grabbed at the opportunity to change the

subject. "She ran away from home and never looked back because of the abuse she suffered at the hands of her father."

"And where was home?" Elsa asked interestedly.

"Portland. In the Rio Grande Valleys on the other side of where my parents lived."

"Really?" Elsa mused. "She said her sister's name was Ivy. This is going to sound completely left field, but my grandmother's name was Ivy. I always perk up when I hear that name."

"Intriguing." Ace murmured, "and she was from Portland too, wasn't she?

"Yep." Elsa nodded.

"What was her maiden name?"

"I don't remember," Elsa frowned, "I think it was Baxter. I am going to have to confirm with aunt Sharla or my cousin, Danica."

"Baxter was Aunt Florence's maiden name," Ace looked at Elsa, "this is intriguing, we may have a little mystery on our hands. What happened to your grandmother?"

"She just abandoned her family, my mother was fifteen when she left, so she had to care for her younger sisters." Elsa said. "Apparently Ivy was abused by her husband, and she couldn't take it anymore, Aunt Sharla said she ran away. Obviously, it was while she was pregnant with Aunt Sara. She must have had Sara at some point and gave her away for adoption and then disappeared from the face of the earth."

"What are you saying?" Ace looked intrigued. "You don't know where she went or what she was up to? This is a small island people don't just vanish."

"Apparently, she did." Elsa frowned. "She went missing forty years ago and hasn't been seen since."

"Well, if your Ivy and Florence's Ivy are the same, let me know how it goes."

"Most def." Elsa nodded. "This would be a major break in the case of the missing grandmother. My cousin, Danica, will be beside herself with this one."

"I like a good mystery too." Ace smiled, "I hope you guys solve this."

"This will be perfect when I send Danica's résumé to Quade. She will be up here, and she can get down to the nitty-gritty of this because I will not have the time. This is great. I am so happy I came by today and heard Florence's story."

"I am happy you came by too," Ace smiled. "Even though you had to tussle with Dorothy."

"Dorothy, who implied that something was wrong with you because you are single?"

"I have often asked myself the same thing." Ace laughed. "It's not from lack of trying. I just have not had any luck in that department."

"Me neither," Elsa grinned. "My last relationship, if you can call it that, was with a mini Toddy. I vowed that I would never ever be with a man like that. I will wait for real love even if I am old and shaky and have no teeth left, and he'd better be faithful or else I am going to castrate him."

Ace laughed heartily. "I can see you doing it too."

"I would," Elsa grinned. "My requirements for a future spouse-boyfriend, or whatever, is for him to be faithful, to be loyal, to be trustworthy, to be truthful, to be loving..."

"I am impressed," Ace whistled. "Those are surprisingly Christian focused requirements, Elsa. It sounds like the fruits of the spirit list right there. From my experience, people in general start with the material aspects of their requirements. You went to the heart of the matter. The very core."

"It's from years of observing one bad relationship after another with my brother." Elsa shrugged. "I realize that lust is fleeting, and that character is what ultimately matters."

"So, the tour is over?" Mason said behind her, "I was just coming to find you guys."

"Yes." Ace nodded. "I am looking forward to seeing what you guys come up with for the PR package."

"I will have it production-ready in three or four weeks," Elsa said guiltily.

Mason was glaring at the two of them as if they had been caught doing something illegal.

Ace chuckled. "Well Elsa, I must say it was nice hanging with you for a few minutes. I just gained a new and unique perspective on relationships. I appreciate that. Maybe we should have some more conversations outside of work?"

Mason was watching her closely. Elsa knew Ace was baiting him. Trying to create some drama.

"Sure," she said brightly.

Ace saluted. "I'll call you. I have to go back to the practice. I am sure Quade will keep me up to date with the times for your presentations."

Elsa watched him walk towards his car and then slowly turned to Mason, who was glaring at her.

"So, how was the tour?" His voice was calm and didn't convey the look in his eye.

"Great." Elsa cleared her throat. "Why are you looking so thunderous?"

"I just overheard your flirtatious conversation with Ace, our client. We don't flirt with clients. "

"I wasn't flirting. If you should know, a resident implied there was something wrong with him for being single. And we had a chat. Totally innocent and above board."

"You were discussing relationships, and you just arranged in front of me to meet with him outside of work." Mason adjusted his glasses. "There are too many things wrong with what just happened."

"He has this theory that you like me." Elsa shrugged. "He was just pulling your leg when he did that."

"I wonder where he would get that notion from?" Mason growled.

"I don't know," Elsa said impatiently, "he is your cousin. You talk to him all the time. Maybe he got it from you."

"No, he didn't," Mason murmured. "I've never discussed you or my feelings for you with Ace."

"I figured." Elsa smiled. "I told him that we don't like each other, and he didn't take me seriously."

"You can't see him outside of work," Mason said grumpily, "so don't make any arrangements in that regard."

"You sound a wee bit jealous, Mr. Magnus." Elsa looked at him and grinned. "Just a tiny bit."

"I am not jealous," Mason said frankly, "and I don't exactly dislike you either."

"Well, good." Elsa nodded. "We are on our way to an understanding. Maybe we can even be friends."

"I don't want to be your friend," Mason said. "I have never wanted to be your friend."

"Okay, so we don't have to be friends," Elsa said faintly. She felt a shaft of disappointment hit her while she said it. "Business acquaintances is fine."

Mason didn't respond to that. He changed the subject abruptly. "It's time to go. We can talk strategy on our way down."

Elsa gritted her teeth. It was not the response she had wanted. She wanted him to tell her what he thought was wrong with her, and why they couldn't be friends. In his perfect little conservative world, he didn't think she was good enough to be his friend.

"What is your relationship with Heather Greyson?" Mason

asked in the silence. She had been silently fuming when he said he didn't want to be her friend. The question caught her off guard.

"Who is Heather Greyson?

"Greyson Industries is our biggest client. Heather is Edmond Greyson's wife. She is quite an influential figure in his life."

"I don't have a clue who she is." Elsa shrugged.

"That's funny, her husband asked specifically about you last night. That's a big deal."

"I may have done an ad for them or something back at my old firm." Elsa glared at him. "Why don't you want to be my friend?"

"You are not ready for the answer to that question." Mason looked at her contemplatively. "When you are ready, we will talk about it.

"Pig," Elsa muttered under her breath.

Mason laughed. "I have heard worse from you."

Chapter Nine

We need to talk, Elsa read the text from Toddy and groaned. She was feeling a little stressed. She had spent the rest of the afternoon acclimatizing herself to the new office. She planned a strategy and tried to haggle with HR for support staff who would work with her on the Golden Acres documentary.

At least she had a fair idea what she was going to do, and she needed to act now while all of those flowers were still in bloom, but everybody was busy, and nobody had any time for the new girl. She had to emphasize that she worked out of Mason Magnus' office to get some of them to move.

She was going to have to win their respect by being the best at what she did.

She called Toddy when she parked before the house. He answered on the first ring.

"Nice of you to tell me that you are working for Mason Magnus," Toddy said before she could say hello.

"Sorry," Elsa sighed. "Today was my first day."

"How was it?" Toddy didn't sound angry at all.

Elsa relaxed a little. "It was good. I got an account to work on, all by my lonesome. I am the boss."

"Is that so?" Toddy chuckled. "I am happy for you. Don't mess it up. You need to show that Magnus guy that you are a Pryce, and you know your stuff."

"Yeah," Elsa chuckled. "You know I was wondering how I was going to break the news to you about working for Mason, but you seem to be taking it well."

"I like the boy," Toddy said. "If I didn't, I wouldn't have practically handed over my company to him—his father's shares or not, I would have put up a fight."

"He doesn't like you though," Elsa muttered. "He has a list of grievances against you a mile long. He said today that if you could come up with an acceptable answer as to why you coveted everything that belonged to his father, he would back off."

Toddy was silent for so long, Elsa had to glance at the phone screen to see if the call was still active.

"Toddy…" She cleared her throat.

"I don't think he wants to hear about our past. I promised his mother I wouldn't say anything to him."

"So, it involves Celine?" Elsa murmured, "I thought so."

"Whatever you are speculating cannot even come close to the truth." Toddy inhaled raggedly.

"Did you have an affair with her, before Manuel died?"

"Celine and I go way back," Toddy said, "way back. Both our families lived in Portland, and they were close."

"That's not answering the question," Elsa said.

Toddy ignored her and kept talking. "I am twenty years older than Celine. When I left the district, she was just a kid. As you know, our father gave me my lump sum, and I came to Kingston and started my business. Admittedly, it wasn't doing so well in the early days. Then just when I was about to give up and do something else, I met this young, ambitious guy named Manuel Magnus.

"He had just left university; he was from a wealthy family with loads of contacts, and he wanted to start an advertising firm. I saw the merits in hitching my cart to his, so I convinced him to join me in my little outfit.

"It was appealing to him. His father was a manufacturer, his mother, a well-known journalist and Manuel was hungry for success on his own terms. He eschewed his family's financial help and decided to go it alone. He was just so driven and had something to prove.

"Mason is a lot like him, in looks and temperament. Manuel didn't know when to slow down and enjoy life."

"So how does Celine come into all this?" Elsa asked.

"She was a family friend, as I said," Toddy paused. "She came to Kingston, I bought her an apartment, sent her to university."

"She was your mistress?" Elsa gasped. "Celine is not the mistress type."

"What is the mistress type?" Toddy chuckled. "And why are you jumping to conclusions? Anyway, after a while, she met my business partner Manuel Magnus."

"He knew that she was your mistress?" Elsa asked.

"I never said she was my mistress," Toddy stressed, "So Manuel fell in love with her, and she dangled that in my face."

"Because you two were in a relationship?" Elsa asked. "Just admit it, Toddy."

"I am not admitting to anything, but I will say I have always loved Celine." Toddy had a coughing bout.

"What's wrong with you?" Elsa was alarmed. She had known Toddy all her life, and she could count on one hand the times that she saw him sick. He was usually healthy as a horse and invincible."

"I have a touch of something. I'll be fine." Toddy choked out. "It's that Mason that is causing my issues. He is stressing me out." Toddy wheezed. "My doctor said I don't need the stress. If I continue this way I just might die."

Toddy had another coughing and hacking jag. That plucked every one of Elsa's heartstrings.

"What is Mason doing to stress you out?" Elsa asked concern gripping her for Toddy. She had always been a little overprotective of him. Shades of her childhood came up to meet her when she thought of all the prayers, she used to pray, begging God to preserve Toddy because she didn't know if she could lose him too.

"Mason is investigating all of my past business deals to discredit my name. He has Cameron Grindley working for him. They don't call Cameron the dirt digger for nothing. And their goal is to dig up dirt on me and see me eat dirt. I can't let it happen." Toddy hardened his voice. "Mason has taken everything from me already. I can't let him take my dignity. I can't let him ruin me."

Elsa sighed. "I don't know much about politics or how it works, but surely Mason doesn't have the power to ruin you."

"He does." Toddy wheezed. "It's only a matter of time before he finds a mistake and then he'll spring it on the public. The prime minister will ask me to resign, and then they'll kick me out of the senate. My reputation in the business world will be mud. I could lose all the money I have, my house, the very clothes on my back."

Toddy coughed. "He will push me off the cliff, and I have no choice but to let go. Maybe the next day, you will find my body in broken little fragments at the bottom."

"My goodness, no," Elsa said feelingly. "That is not going

to happen. I'll talk to him."

"It won't make a difference," Toddy sounded like he was struggling to breathe. "He has to want something more than he wants revenge."

"Like what?" Elsa breathed. "What could Mason want more than revenge?"

"Love." Toddy hacked. "I want you to marry him." He finally came back on the phone, his voice sounding raspy.

"What did you say?" Elsa asked in shock.

"I am going to make him an offer he can't refuse. I am going to offer him you. In exchange, he leaves me alone with no Cameron rifling around in my past, I'll be safe."

"Have you lost your mind!" Elsa bellowed. "Which century is this again?"

"Are you scared that he will throw my offer back in the face?" Toddy asked weakly. "He has to choose, you or revenge on me."

"I am not that important to Mason," Elsa growled. "Besides, I don't want to marry him in some kind of business exchange. I don't want to marry anybody at all. When I do, it will be for love and compatibility and all the right reasons."

"Well then, I am over the cliff," Toddy said his voice woebegone. "It was just a suggestion anyway. I should go, I just coughed up blood. I just might die before Mason finishes me off."

"Toddy!" Real fear gripped Elsa, but Toddy had hung up the phone.

Elsa frantically dialed Myrna's number instead.

Myrna's phone went to voice mail.

****

Giselle and Tiana were laughing and talking when she got

in. Tiana was in the middle of describing her wedding plans, and Giselle was studiously listening.

"You look weird," Giselle said when she walked in." Don't tell me you got fired on your first day."

"No," Elsa frowned, "I just got off the phone with Toddy. He was complaining that Mason was after him and that he was hanging off a cliff with no support."

"What else is new," Tiana snorted. "This feud between Toddy and Mason is old and tiring."

"Tonight he sounded like he was clutching the last straw though," Elsa kicked off her shoes, "He was coughing, said he was coughing up blood, and then hung up."

"Say what?" Giselle grabbed her phone. "I need to call Myrna."

"Already called. She isn't answering." Elsa pulled her blouse from her skirt.

"Well then, we need to call Lincoln," Giselle muttered, "and we need to get over there."

"I agree." Tiana nodded.

"At least let me have a quick shower." Elsa headed upstairs. "I feel like I need to wash this day off, and I have a niggling feeling that Toddy is not as bad as he sounded. He was blackmailing me."

"Why?" Tiana asked, appalled at her casual attitude.

"Because he proposed that he was going to offer me to Mason Magnus in exchange for Mason to leave him alone. I feel as if one or two of his coughs were exaggerated."

"Oh," Tiana widened her eyes.

Giselle, who was dialing a number, paused. "You didn't say he was hallucinating."

"He wasn't." Elsa headed up the stairs. "He was coughing and hacking, but he was lucid. He made it clear. If I didn't help him, he would lose everything. Not just his senate seat, but his reputation, his standing in the community, yadda yadda yadda…"

"Help him as is in become Mason's wife?" Giselle asked her slowly as if she was just patching it together in her head.

"That's right." Elsa nodded.

"So Mason has something on him?" Tiana asked, confused. "Is Toddy into something illegal?"

"I don't know," Elsa wrinkled her brow. "The conversation I just had was quite strange."

"Let's just say Toddy is into something illegal, and Mason is holding it over him. Why would Mason take him up on such a preposterous offer?" Giselle asked agitated, "and why would you be a party to this emotional blackmail."

"Because I am the only single one. You are married to Pete, Tiana is getting married soon, and I am single." Elsa gripped the rail and slumped on the staircase. She looked at her sisters through the balustrade. "There is a disadvantage to being the single one. I am the only one available to take one for the team."

"You are the only one who Mason would consider giving up his revenge for anyway." Tiana smirked, "whether the three of us were single or not. You have always been Mason Magnus' favorite. You and he had an exclusive thing going on."

"No!" Elsa frowned. "What we had was more like mutual dislike."

"I wonder what it could be that Mason has on Toddy?" Tiana asked fearfully. "Did he kill someone? Steal something?"

"I don't know." Elsa covered her face. "And I don't think Toddy will tell me. He doesn't even want to tell me what went down between him and Celine before she got married to Mason's father. And something went down, he paid her way through university, and he bought her an apartment."

"That's what he does for his mistresses," Tiana said and then widened her eyes. "Ooh…"

"Yep." Elsa sighed. "My thoughts exactly."

"Go bathe, we should go check on him," Giselle said. "Let me call Lincoln and tell him about Toddy, he will call the others."

Elsa had a shower in record time. She pulled on her jeans and a t-shirt and was on her way downstairs while Giselle was on the phone with Lincoln.

Giselle hung up. "Lincoln is already over there. He says Myrna called Grace as soon as she heard Toddy hacking and coughing. Grace said he has aspiration pneumonia. He must have inhaled food, stomach acid, or saliva into his lungs. He has difficulty breathing now, but they'll be carrying him to Sunrise Medical shortly."

"Will he be okay?" Elsa whispered.

"I think so." Giselle nodded. "They caught it fast. Let's go meet them at Sunrise Medical. I'll drive."

****

The drive over was solemn.

"I can't imagine life without Toddy," Tiana said, sniffing. "He is not perfect, but he was the only one in all our families that took us in when we had no one. He saved us from foster care. He sent us to the best schools. He treated us like little Princesses."

"He gave us a lump sum of money when we reached twenty-one," Giselle murmured, "I mean, who does that?"

"He taught me how to drive." Elsa was sitting in the back seat with tears in her eyes. "He was the reason I fell in love with the ad world. One day I was in the kitchen moping about Giselle's good grades and Tiana's tight attachment to

Yara. I was feeling like the odd man out as usual, and Toddy said, 'Start comparing yourself to yourself and no one else. I know you are a part of a triplet, but you are going to have to forget what your sisters have and where they are. You are not walking in their shoes, but you will never be comfortably walking on your own if you keep comparing yourself to them. Focus on you, Elsa.'"

"He said that?" Tiana turned around and looked at her tears in her eyes, "You compared yourself to me and thought I was better?"

"Yes." Elsa nodded.

"That's funny." Tiana laughed and then wiped the tears from her eyes, "Of the three of us, you always seemed to be the one who seemed to have it all together."

"Georgia calls her the fun one," Giselle said dryly. "I am the boring one, Tiana, the middle of the road, and you are the gloriously fun one. The one that lives her life on her own terms."

"If only that were true," Elsa snorted. "Maybe I am just the secretive one. The one who appears to be having a whale of a time, and yet inside I am howling with despair."

"What are you saying?" Giselle turned into the private hospital's parking lot and shut the car off. "Are you depressed or something?"

"I am saying," Elsa sighed, "I have my share of issues. Some of them I hide. Tiana has been psychoanalyzing me. She knows what I am talking about."

"You mean about Mason?" Tiana frowned. "I was right?"

"Yup." Elsa nodded. "Four years ago, I went to his apartment and I…"

Giselle and Tiana looked at her with shock.

"And you…" Tiana prompted. "Don't leave us hanging, woman. Don't tell me I am the only virgin sitting in this car. What about staying away from penises and waiting for a commitment to a loyal man?"

"I was half-drunk from Myrna's homemade wine. We were talking about Mason, and she was saying that he had a fiancée, a lovely girl, Anna Kay."

"And you got jealous," Tiana murmured, "like you always do when Mason talks to anybody else."

"Let her finish," Giselle whispered. "I don't want her to stop talking."

Elsa chuckled. "I should leave you hanging."

"No, God no." Giselle shook her head. "So, you found out about Anna Kay and then…"

"I asked Myrna where Mason's apartment was. Of course, she knew the address. You know she and Mason are as tight as thieves, and he bought this new apartment which was close to his business."

"So I left the house. Drove downtown to the apartment. I told the security I was Mason Magnus' fiancée Anna Kay and he let me in after calling Mason. It turned out Mason was home."

"Ooh," Tiana grinned.

"I showed up at his apartment door. I had on my backless red dress, you know the one. Gis borrowed it last year for her date night with Pete."

"Yep. That slut dress," Tiana said disdainfully. "Can I borrow it?"

Elsa chuckled. "Ask Gis, I haven't gotten it back."

"It's gone, threw it in the trash," Gis said ruefully, "Pete ripped it off me in true caveman style, we barely made it inside the …"

Giselle looked at Tiana's widening eyes and Elsa's grinning face. "My husband and I can't get enough of each other. But we digress, we were talking about you."

"Where was I?" Elsa frowned.

"You went to Mason's door in a red slut dress to seduce him," Tiana said helpfully.

"Yes. So when Mason came to the door, looking all fine and serious. I said, surprise!"

"What did he do?" Giselle reached for a pack of gum and passed it around.

"Is it sugar-free?" Elsa asked.

"No," Tiana snorted. "This girl acts like sugar is a drug."

"I am going to muzzle you, Tiana Pryce," Giselle growled. "No interruptions."

"Sorray." Tiana chuckled.

"And what did Mason say?" Giselle prompted her.

"Mason said, 'You are not Anna Kay.' And I said, 'No, I am better than Anna Kay.' He stepped back from the door. I walked into his apartment and looked around. I gushed at the view. And he said, 'What do you want, Elsa?' and I said, 'I want you to make love to me.'"

Tiana gasped and then covered her mouth.

"And then I walked up to him and kissed him, and he kissed me back. And we had one of those passionate clinches where everywhere he touched felt electric, and we ended up on the settee and then…"

"Whew chile," Giselle fanned her face. "Go on."

"And then he pulled away from me and said, 'Elsa, what on earth are we doing?'"

"And I said, 'This is a long time in the making, I want to be with you just once. I want you to be my first.'"

"And then he shook his head and backed away and mumbled something about this is not how he envisioned us together. He is engaged and loved somebody else and that I should leave."

"That's it?" Giselle whispered cautiously.

"Yup." Elsa nodded. "Thwarted again by Mason Magnus. He did ask me if I wanted to talk. I was so pissed, I told him no and left."

"I know that Mason doesn't like me and is not attracted to me in the slightest. So I am not sure what Toddy hopes to gain from this whole scenario, if he suggests to Mason that he marry me, Mason will laugh him out of the building, but if it makes Toddy feel better I am going to tell him yes, offer me to Mason as a sacrificial lamb."

"It wouldn't be a sacrifice," Tiana grinned. "You have had a thing for Mason for too long now. Maybe Toddy is doing you a favor."

"First of all," Elsa growled, "I am not a charity case. I don't want Toddy to force Mason to marry me. I will tell Toddy yes, I'll do whatever it takes to keep him happy, but when he approaches Mason with this absurd idea, Mason will say no."

"What if he says yes?" Giselle asked. "He might say yes, it's not impossible. He has always had a thing for you too Elsa. And he was right in not having sex with you unprotected, without commitment, and while he was engaged to another woman. Mason has always been a stand-up kind of guy. Admit it, you secretly respect him for it."

"She doesn't admire that," Tiana snorted. "What she wanted was for him to ravish her and lose control. She's sick for real."

"You always defend Mason," Elsa glared at Tiana, "I am sorry I told you about four years ago."

"I am happy you told me," Tiana glared right back, "because I am going to give you a little piece of advice from experience. I was in a similar situation. Men like Mason prefer maturity. You have always approached Mason like you are a juvenile delinquent. You can't appeal to him that way, insults and acting like a temptress won't work. Be your lovely self, let him get to know you, appeal to his head, as well as his lower part."

"Amen," Giselle murmured. "I feel that."

"Enough about Mason and me." Elsa opened the car door. "I was so distracted by everything I didn't even tell you that I met Florence Jackson."

Chapter Ten

As usual, Elsa's alarm clock went off at six o'clock on the dot.

She showered and got ready for the day, a low humming depression dogging her footsteps even when she entered the Magnus Communication building.

Mason was in office when she got there, and she thought she would have been early. His secretary Callie was there as well, sipping coffee and reading the paper.

"Hey," her eyes brightened when she saw Elsa, "I never got a chance to officially welcome you yesterday." She got up and shook Elsa's hand."

"HR will be sending up your assistant today."

"Thank you, Callie." Elsa nodded. "Is Mason available?"

"Not yet, he has been on that phone call for a while."

"Okay then," Elsa turned to go to her office. There were a million and one things to do to make an advertising campaign come together, and she was a party of one. She was really going to need an assistant.

Callie cleared her throat. "About your assistant…"

Elsa spun around again, "yes?"

"She is not the best fit," Callie was whispering, "I know you and Mason go way back, and you may have some influence."

"Who told you that?" Elsa frowned.

"He had a picture with you and your sisters on his desk from that ad you did for the chip company. You were adorable little girls."

"Thank you." Elsa smiled. "I remember that ad. Toddy was the one who cast us for it. It was three different flavors of tortillas. Giselle was honey barbecue; Tiana was ranch, and I was spicy. He had it framed and in his office."

"Well, Mason inherited it and kept it on his desk for years. He only recently removed it." Callie looked at her, puzzled. "I was told to show him any references to you in the papers. I keep up with all your ad work too."

"Mason kept track of me?" Elsa murmured. "No wonder my interview was so easy."

"Yes, he does," Callie said. "I report everything I find."

"Does he track Giselle and Tiana too?" Elsa asked curiously.

"No." Callie looked at her quizzically. "They are not in the advertising business, are they?"

"Oh, no." Elsa shook her head, feeling stupid. So that was why Mason was tracking her. She was looking for a little ray of hope for Toddy. He had seemed so pathetic last night, unable to talk with the gas mask over his face to help him breathe. He didn't even look well enough to be challenging Mason for anything, even though the doctors had reassured them that Toddy could recover in mere weeks and be as good as new.

"Anyway," Callie cleared her throat. "The assistant that

HR is sending up is Iris. She filled in for me twice when I went on maternity leave. She is a good worker. I doubt you'll have any problems with that, but I really didn't want her back up here on the seventh floor."

"Why?" Elsa asked.

"Let me just come out and say it. I am not one to gossip and hide around corners, but Iris is unprofessional when it comes to Mason."

"How so?" Elsa asked, widening her eyes.

"You'll find out," Callie said. "I am just giving you fair warning. She is attending school and apparently used to be a stripper or is a stripper, I don't know. When it comes to Mason, she is unfirable."

"A stripper? Unfirable?" Elsa frowned.

"I heard she worked in one of those places uptown. What's it called again, Jaded. The club where they do bad, bad things. That is where Mason found her. However, the story goes, this Iris girl has great weight with him for some reason. Granted, I can see that she is pretty, but no matter what she does, she gets a pass."

Elsa looked at Callie, shocked. "She has a relationship with Mason?"

"I don't know if they have a current relationship, but I wish they were not sending her back up here, maybe you can change that?" Callie asked eagerly.

"We'll see how it works out," Elsa said, a shard of jealousy hitting her out of nowhere.

She went back to her office worried about this Iris, who had greater weight with Mason than her. It wasn't shaping up to be a stellar start to the day, and she couldn't handle that latest development now.

****

Mason spent most of his morning in meetings, as usual. He had forgotten to have lunch and was taking a late lunch with Cameron, in the dining room.

The place was mostly empty except for Elsa, and Frederick, the production director who was huddled over a computer. They were so deep in watching what was on the screen they hadn't even looked up when he walked in.

Mason smiled slightly. Elsa had been working for him for an entire week and a half, and he had rarely seen her. She had given him brief updates twice in the mornings so far, and she had been brisk and efficient. When she was focused, she was focused, and he had to admire that.

She was quite professional and kept him at arm's length as he had requested. That's what he wanted. So why was he feeling slightly troubled about it?

He found himself thinking about her at odd times in the day, and he found errands to run so that he could pass her office when she was there.

She had spent most of the last week at Golden Acres producing the documentary, but now she was back.

She had the production department on their toes.

"She's good," Frederick had told him just yesterday. "She knows what she wants, and for the most part, she is right."

It would be nice if she wanted him, Mason thought wistfully. As soon as the thought crossed his mind he slammed it down. He had weaned himself off of those thoughts years ago.

"Who's that?" Cameron followed his gaze and then whistled. "She is pretty."

Elsa looked up at the same time, and their eyes met.

She waved and then looked back down at the screen when

Frederick pointed something out to her.

"You like her." Cameron chuckled.

Mason dragged his eyes from Elsa's side of the room. "That's Elsa Pryce."

"One of Toddy's triplet sisters?" Cameron groaned. "Are you serious?"

Mason nodded. "My mother asked me to hire her."

"Your mother?" Cameron mocked. "Your mother couldn't get you to do anything you don't want to do, and you know it."

Mason glared at Cameron but was prevented from answering when the dining room staff served them lunch.

"You do know that we are very close to moving on Toddy, don't you?" Cameron whispered, "I can't believe you have his sister working with you. That's the sister he is closest to, the one that is in advertising. He is always bragging that she is a miniature him. I thought you wanted to crush him, to destroy him?"

"I do." Mason glanced at Elsa again and then back down at his food. He hadn't forgotten their conversation when she had told him that he was fighting in a war that he knew nothing about. Since the day she had said it, the thought had been digging in his mind like a bur.

"Does she know that you want to drive her brother into the ground?"

"Yes," Mason tucked into his food. "You should eat up."

Cameron started eating, but he was watching Mason as he pretended that he wasn't highly in tune with everything that the Pryce girl was doing across the room.

Elsa looked up twice, maybe because she felt Mason's laser focus on her, and she stared at him too.

The two of them weren't fooling anybody. Cameron almost laughed out loud. He wondered if they were lovers. It certainly seemed like it. Mason's expression was shuttered, but his eyes were blazing all sorts of emotions when he stared at her.

"I don't know, Mason. This feels like a trap. This is Toddy's doing, somehow. I told you he was good."

"I don't see how Elsa working here has anything to do with Toddy." Mason raised an eyebrow. "She busted Geo King's nose when he made a pass at her and was fired. No matter how good Toddy is, he couldn't have seen that coming."

"I think it's his counter-strategy," Cameron whispered. "Give her a wide berth, or else you are going to lose this war with Toddy and operation bring-Toddy-to-his-knees is over."

"She has nothing to do with this." Mason spared a slice of tomato and glared at Cameron. "You are paranoid if you believe Toddy is some sort of super strategist. He is old and tired and just recovering from the pneumonia that put him in the hospital."

"He is as tough as nails; the pneumonia bit was not a setback. Never underestimate an old veteran." Cameron cleared his throat. "I have my detectives digging up all sorts of sordid details about Toddy Pryce. His personal life makes for quite an interesting complicated and salacious read, that man epitomizes the term alley cat, and he has just as many lives."

"I know. What about his business interests, found anything else amiss? I want something to dig my teeth in, something that can make a splash," Mason said, savoring the thought, "I don't just want to bring him down. I don't just want him politically gone, and maybe humiliated in the business circles. I want him in jail."

"Jail?" Cameron murmured. "I can't promise jail, but there is a whisper about something. Toddy will lose everything if it is proven that he was associated with a particular business. There are other things worse than jail, you know. The thing I am looking into, if it pans out will be a blow to his reputation."

"Apart from that, there is nothing else. Toddy has toed the line many times but has not crossed it from what I'm finding so far." Cameron murmured. "But I'll keep looking. If you want to bury him, we'll bury him."

Chapter Eleven

"**W**hile you were away," Iris placed a few memos on Elsa's desk. "Your cousin Danica called. She said she has landed, and that Guy picked her up at the airport. She says she would be staying with him at his farm for a few days."

"Good, thank you." Elsa sighed. "I was wondering how I was going to get to the airport and then get back here for filming."

Iris grunted and sat across from Elsa and stared at her unblinkingly.

Elsa looked at her, searching in her overcrowded overworked brain as to why.

"Do we have a meeting?"

"I penciled it into your appointment book. You wanted a brainstorming session for the best places to find wealthy older people." Iris said it without expression, and Elsa closed her eyes.

Iris obviously disliked her. It wasn't anything she said, the girl was superefficient, but Elsa could feel the dislike rolling off her in waves.

She hadn't had the time over the last week to address why the 'unfirable' Iris disliked her. She didn't know anything about her really, except that Iris dressed nicely. She had some pieces in her wardrobe that Elsa would wear.

She was efficient, she gave excellent suggestions, and she was pretty. She was always looking flawless, and she wore her natural hair in a giant curly puff. Elsa almost asked if it was real.

Luckily, she was saved from that mistake when one of Mason's clients had asked. The poor woman had been treated to a cold yes.

Elsa had noted quite readily that Iris was not into personal observations or small talk, especially about her hair. She was there to do her job and only that. She seemed to keep out of Callie's way, and she didn't venture near Mason's office.

Iris was now sitting before Elsa's desk. The clock indicating that it was exactly four-thirty.

Elsa sighed. "I didn't remember Iris."

She rubbed her temples. I have to do a quick run-up to Golden Acres with Tony to capture some evening footage. I want a good transition from morning to evening. I asked him to do it by himself, and it wasn't what I wanted, so I have to go this evening and give him some direction.

"That's okay, I already made a list," Iris said, "and I compiled the budget and did the forecast for each option."

"You did?" Elsa smiled. "Thank you so much, you are the absolute best."

"Just doing my job," Iris said, a little emotion leaking into her voice. "I like working with you."

"You do?" Elsa asked, her mouth half-opened. "I thought you disliked me."

"Oh no, far from that," Iris widened her eyes. "I was just trying my best to be ultra-professional," Iris said. "Callie said I was not professional the last time I was up here."

Elsa cleared her throat. "Well, she did tell me that you didn't act professional around Mason and that you were a stripper and unfirable."

"That's ridiculous." Iris chuckled. "She hated that I did a good job in her absence and that Mason didn't miss her when she went away the last time. I made sure of it. I set out to be the best assistant he had ever had. Callie was just jealous. As for me being a stripper, my sister is one, we look very much alike, I told Callie this when she was making her innuendos. I have no time after working here to be a stripper. This is a demanding place, and I want a promotion."

"Professional jealousy." Elsa exhaled slowly. And there she was imagining all different sorts of scenarios with Iris and Mason meeting at a strip club.

She should have known better; Mason did not frequent strip clubs or night clubs or anything of that sort.

Maybe that was what Callie wanted her to think. When she was in a less crowded frame of mind, she would unpack their conversation again and wonder if that was the reaction that Callie wanted from her, but for now she focused on Iris and smiled tiredly. "How much work do you think you can handle?"

"Bring it on," Iris said solemnly.

Elsa was on her way out the door when she met up with Mason.

"Miss Pryce," he said smoothly. "You seem to be in a hurry."

"I have to meet Tony at Golden Acres for footage." Elsa rummaged in her bag for one of her sugar-free snack bars. She had gone to the cafeteria for lunch and had ended up not eating. She found one and took it out. "I am going to have to eat and drive."

"What a coincidence," Mason said dryly, "I am going that way, you can eat while I drive.

"I won't argue." Elsa grimaced. "I feel a headache coming on. No doubt caused by hunger.

"Will it take long?" Mason pressed the elevator button to the underground parking lot and turned to her.

"No." Elsa shook her head, "I just want footage from the start of dinner, some shots of some delicious food. I also want some night spa footage. Some residents only do night spa; it helps them sleep. The spa manager said that they have an insomnia cure rate of near a hundred percent. I think that should be a selling point. The insomnia rate for older adults is near sixty percent."

"I spoke to one resident who said the one reason that made him move to Golden Acres was the sleep. He hadn't slept for more than two hours a night for close to ten years, and then he moved to Golden Acres. The various activities and especially the night spa, helped him so much he doesn't need his eye medication anymore."

"You don't say." Mason mused. "I wouldn't have thought of appealing to that aspect of the place."

"I did my research," Elsa said. "After speaking to almost all the residents, the one thing that keeps coming up is the quality sleep they get at Golden Acres. I think more than anything, the people I have talked to seem to value a good night's rest without medication. I have to play it up in the infomercial."

"You accomplished quite a bit in your week and a half," Mason said. "And you'll be ready with this by the end of next week, you said?"

"Oh, yes." Elsa nodded. "I have been micromanaging

the footage. I am going to need a shorter version of this for television and other visual locations. There is no need to shoot twice."

"Next is the interviews with the instructors and the doctors and the administrators and the residents themselves. I'll do that myself. I have a pretty nice camera for it. I'll do some editing and then give it to the production department to clean up. I squeezed the interviews in for all of next week. So I won't be here."

"You should stay at my place in the hills then," Mason said, "so that you don't have to drive back and forth every day."

"Your place?" Elsa widened her eyes. "You have a place in the hills?"

"Yes," Mason nodded. "Did I forget to mention it?"

"I am pretty sure you did," Elsa nodded, "you only said that Quade lives up here when we were passing his place."

"We are practically neighbors." Mason shrugged. "I loved going up to visit him in the hills, and then the land beside him became available a couple of years ago. I bought it and built myself a villa and two cottages. One for my housekeeper, the other for my mother."

"Oh," Elsa opened her mouth and then snapped it shut. "Well then, I'll take you up on your kind offer to stay…"

"No, it's just practical." Mason said, "Golden Acres is a stone's throw away from there, you can walk to work. Set up your camera and do your interviews. I actually envy you for it. I don't spend enough time at Hibiscus Lodge."

"That's the name of your place?" Elsa asked.

"Yes, my mother named it. You'll see why." Mason chuckled. "She had a dinner-plate hibiscus craze once, and she used my garden to indulge herself. She joined the Horticultural Society at her cousin Celia's request, and they went crazy in my garden."

"Celia, Ace's mother." Elsa asked. "I didn't know she was the flower-loving type."

"She loves gardening."

Elsa chuckled. "And apparently she loves gardeners. I heard through family gossip that Ace may actually be a Wiley. You know Micky Wiley was Celia and Ace Senior's gardener and allegedly Celia's lover."

"I heard that too," Mason frowned at her. "I chalked it up to ridiculous family gossip. Celia would never cheat on her husband."

"Oh, really?" Elsa raised an eyebrow. "You shouldn't swear for people. In my opinion, anybody is capable of anything."

Mason shook his head. "That's the issue I have with family gossip and gossip in general. You take one bit of information, and then you run with it as if it is real."

"Every family gossips," Elsa frowned, "doesn't yours?"

"I have been too busy to hear what the latest gossip topics are in my family." Mason frowned. "We are pretty fractured on my father's side. There is no family get-together or anything like that. My grandparents had two sons. They are both dead. My father had me, my uncle had Garret, who is as non-gossipy as they come. He is busy, I am busy, years go by before we see each other.

"My grandparents emigrated to Canada years ago. They have many family members up there. I don't know many of them. So even if there was gossip, I wouldn't care."

"But on your mother's side," Elsa's eyes twinkled. "You have more than enough family to make up for that. Tell me more about them." Elsa searched in her bag for her bottled water.

"My great grandfather, Ray Walker, was a meteorologist. And he named all of his children from major hurricanes.

My great grandmother's name was Sunny, he was Ray, and then he had all these hurricanes. I kid you not, they had a local band called, Sunny Ray and the Hurricanes they were popular at wakes."

Elsa chuckled. "Really? They had a sense of humor."

"Yes, they did. I wish I knew them." Mason shrugged. "They both died before I was born. Anyway, they had one boy and six girls. The lone boy, Charlie, was my mother's father. He died when he was just seventeen in a freak swimming accident. He had gotten a girl in the district pregnant before he died, and she was even younger. So my great grandparents quietly took the child when she was born and raised her as their own.

"That child was my mom; she grew up with six aunts. She was a year younger than her youngest aunt, Celine, and they were very close—are very close."

"I see." Elsa nodded. "So, they keep each other's secrets?"

"Something like that." Mason glanced at her. "Are you trying to imply something?"

"Well." Elsa shrugged. "They both seem to have a colorful past. Your mother and Toddy, Ace's mother, and Micky Wiley."

"That district in Portland is a hotbed of secrets and drama." Mason drove out of the parking garage. "I am not surprised that they keep each other's secrets."

"Toddy said he knew your family long before Kingston. He said the Pryces and the Walkers were very close."

"I just bet they were," Mason murmured.

"Doesn't that surprise you?" Elsa asked fishing to see how much he knew about his mother and Toddy's past.

"No," Mason said. "It is a small district, so I am not shocked that they knew each other."

"I would want to know if I were you," Elsa murmured.

"I've been thinking the same lately and I am doing something about it," Mason said cryptically.

"I asked Toddy the other night." Elsa confessed, "and he said he promised your mother not to tell you anything about it. Maybe you could ask him, talk to him. I am hoping there is still time for you to pull back in your pursuit of revenge. Toddy said you might have information on him that could sink him."

"Oh, I do," Mason grunted. "Toddy deserves everything that is coming to him, Elsa."

"Even though he is sick," Elsa gasped. "He is not well."

"He is getting better," Mason said. "I have no sympathy for him. You see him as the brother that saved your life. I see him as the man that destroyed mine. He should pay for what he did to me, to my mother, to my family. Revenge is a dish best served cold. I have been waiting to get Toddy and now I almost have him. I am not giving that up."

Elsa shuddered. "And nothing can stop you, can it?"

"No." Mason glanced at her. "Nothing."

Chapter Twelve

Mason waited in the parking lot for Elsa while she flitted from one area of Golden Acres to the other. She knew what kind of footage she wanted, and Tony and his crew obeyed her directives without complaint.

When they were finished shooting, it was a little past eight o'clock that evening and Mason was ravenously hungry. He hadn't had anything to eat for most of the day. He had been out the door heading to dinner at his favorite eatery in New Kingston when he had seen Elsa and decided on the spur of the moment to drive with her up here.

Offering her his place to stay at Hibiscus Lodge had also been an impulse decision. He had wanted to be in her company. It was just like old times. He had found himself visiting Toddy's house not to see his mother, but to see Elsa. She was fascinating, even when they were just trading barbs with each other.

He called his housekeeper, Dotty, while he was on his way

to the villa to tell her he was stopping by for dinner with a friend. Dotty was elated. She liked it when he dropped by on weekdays so she could showcase her culinary prowess.

Elsa opened the car door and sighed loudly. "I got what I wanted. I have to be grateful for that, but boy, am I hungry."

Mason nodded. "Well, let's go. My housekeeper said she has prepared a spread."

Elsa chuckled. "You are hungry, too, huh?"

"Yep." Mason nodded. "That is why I am grateful that the lodge is near here. It's just five minutes uphill."

Elsa's phone rang, and she squealed. "Welcome to Jamaica, Danica! I can't wait to see you!"

By the time she was in mid-conversation, Mason was turning into the Italian cypress-lined driveway.

"This place is gorgeous," Elsa turned to him and covered the phone. "I was expecting a wooden cabin kind of situation, rustic and quaint."

She looked at the two-story building and then out at the view of the city lights. "You even have a view. Wow, I am impressed."

Mason chuckled.

The lights were all blazing on the inside. Dotty met him at the door.

"Mr. Magnus!" She grinned at him. "I placed everything in warmers on the upstairs deck. I figured you and your company would like the view.

Mason nodded. "Thanks Dotty. This is Elsa. She will be staying here next week. Tonight I am just giving her a taste of the place."

Dotty looked at him, shocked for a second, and then recovered. He never carried women to the lodge. It was his sacred space.

"If I knew I would have lit some candles." Dotty grinned

like a Cheshire cat. "But I guess the area is still intimate. I could turn off the floodlights at the back, leave on the softer lights and the firepit…"

"Dotty," Mason said, exasperated, "stop, she is just a friend, not even that, a coworker."

He was glad that Elsa was finishing up her conversation with her cousin and had not heard a word.

When Elsa came off the phone, Dotty shook Elsa's hand enthusiastically like she was a long-lost prodigal just finding her way home. She couldn't be more obvious if she tried.

"I have left everything out that you will need," Dotty said. "Don't bother to wash up. I'll be over first thing in the morning."

She left hurriedly, scurrying to the back door and to one of the two guest cottages that was about a half-mile from the main house.

He had bought the two-bedroom cottages with the land, and he had fixed them up first. His mother had claimed one, and Rufus and Dotty lived in the other.

Mason sighed. He expected that Dotty and Rufus would speculate about the latest turn of events tonight.

He could imagine Dotty gushing to Rufus about him bringing home a female.

"I love the décor!" Elsa declared, looking around. "It feels like I've seen this place before."

"So, you don't remember that you chose it." Mason raised an eyebrow.

"I did, when?" Elsa looked around her mouth opened.

"I left my personal copy of Caribbean Styles with Myrna a couple years ago; it was the edition where they featured rustic-chic resorts or something like that. You took it from Myrna, chose your favorite rooms, made notes on my book, and turned over the ears on my pages. I just happened to like the ones you liked too. So I recreated it here.

Elsa opened her mouth. "Those weren't notes."

Mason grinned, "Oh, they weren't?"

"I knew it was your copy of the magazine. I made up a narrative about you and your future wife. What I wrote was so lewd. I wanted you to read it and be shocked and disgusted and confront me about my thoughts and how unbecoming it was for a girl yadda yadda. You never said a thing."

"I know." Mason grinned. "I realized quite early that you would do anything for my attention if I reacted in one way or the other the game would be over."

"You thought we were playing a game?" Elsa asked.

"Oh yes," Mason said softly. "You were a lonely teenage girl testing out her sexual prowess on me, and I was the stoic reluctant admirer who wouldn't give you the time of day. We were locked into that narrative. None of us wanting to break our roles or reveal how we really felt until four years ago."

"How did you really feel?" Elsa swallowed.

"You know how I felt," Mason said, "I told you."

"You said that you were disgusted with my assault on you," Elsa cleared her throat. "And that I was still acting like an immature nymphomaniac."

"That was after I told you that I wanted a real relationship, and you laughed in my face." Mason grimaced. "You deserved that speech."

"Maybe I did." Elsa headed for a portrait of his father. Obviously trying to get her thoughts together, trying to ignore the familiar tension between them. She would change the topic soon enough; he was getting too deep. Whenever Elsa had any soul searching to do, she usually changed the topic quickly to deflect.

He didn't have long to wait.

"Your dad was handsome. He had a handlebar mustache.

You should try one."

"I hear that kind of facial hair tickles when you get close to a woman." Mason shook his head. "Clean-shaven is what I like. I think it would be more comfortable for me and my partner.

She glanced at him shyly when he said that which was interesting. Elsa had never been bashful in his presence, and that may be because he had changed the rules of their game, by saying out loud what was between them.

He turned on the stereo. He had on Dennis Brown, of course. The music would play upstairs on the patio because of the speakers up there. Coincidentally the song For You came on.

It was his favorite song of all time. He had fond memories of his father singing it to his mom, and Mason vowed that he would sing it to some worthy woman one day. Somehow, he had always pictured that worthy woman to be Elsa. He had always harbored a little fantasy that she would grow up and stop playing with him. He had given her ample time to do so.

He leaned on the pillar and waited patiently while Elsa walked around the open concept living room area and gushed about different focal points.

He found it ironic that she was right here, right now in the space that she had earmarked and called his love den. He had gotten the magazine from his mother. She gave him copies of her magazines all the time. He had left it on the kitchen counter after a visit, and Myrna had put it up for him. Elsa must have heard it was his and decided to write her scandalous little stories, all of them starring him and some woman that he couldn't handle. Her stories had centered around the pictures that she liked.

She had liked the relaxed décor styles with the white and beige walls and the dark brown bamboo floors and the exposed wood beams. Stories aside, he had liked the décor too and had decided to follow the style when he built this place.

He never forgot anything that Elsa did or said, that had always been his problem.

"I am so sorry." She looked across at him, contritely. "You are hungry, and here I am acting like a tourist in your living room."

"Well, come on then," Mason said lightly. He had forgotten his hunger anyway. "Dotty has the food upstairs on the covered patio."

"Who did that painting?" She pointed to a landscape view of his backyard.

"Rufus, Dotty's husband." Mason headed up the stairs.

"It is good." Elsa followed. "And that's your backyard?"

"Yes, that's the back of the house. All of these are his," Mason said when they walked up the stairs. He specializes in landscapes. He did all of the paintings at Golden Acres too. He started out as my gardener, but now he is too busy for me."

"I am happy for him. For years he toiled away at his craft with only me as his customer."

They entered the upstairs deck where the food was laid out. The night was bordering on cold, but Dotty had lit the firepit.

"It's er...romantic up here." Elsa turned to him, surprise in her eyes. "The view, the fire, the food...the food smells wonderful."

"It does smell lovely," Mason said quickly. "This is all a coincidence though, there was no romance intended."

Elsa chuckled. "Don't worry, I'll not read anything in it, even though that Dennis Brown song, For You seems like it is playing on loop."

"It probably is," Mason grinned. "I am a true fan, I had it on repeat last time I was here."

"For you, there is no cup I would not full, no string I would not pull, for you," Elsa sang and twirled. She grinned at Mason. "I want this song played at my wedding, and I want the man to mean it."

"Every single word. And then I'll sing it back to him because I am not getting married without meaning every word. I think this is a true love song."

Mason stared at her in the half-light, finding himself transfigured by her beauty. He suddenly had the insane urge to be the man that was the recipient of her song.

He had to visibly pull himself from that treacherous thought.

"My father sang it to my mother at their wedding," Mason said huskily. "He said he meant every word of it too."

"He really did love her, didn't he?" Elsa's voice was sad. She headed for the food warmers and filled her plate, he followed suit.

"But it wasn't equal," he said after a while. "I have been thinking about my parents' marriage since you told me that I should get the back story. I finally took off my rose-tinted glasses."

"And?" Elsa raised an eyebrow.

"Maybe I saw things the way I wanted to see them," Mason admitted aloud. "My dad did work a lot and spent a good chunk of his time away from home. My mother sometimes looked sad and lonely."

"Everything wasn't perfect, was it?" Elsa said cryptically. "I wonder what else wasn't as it seems."

"What do you know?" Mason asked solemnly. "You talked to Toddy, what did he say?"

Elsa avoided looking at him. "Well…"

"Whatever he told you, my dad was not presented in the best light, I am sure," Mason growled.

"I think you should talk to Toddy yourself." Elsa spared a chunk of sweet potato and contemplated it. "Have you ever really talked to him about this whole stupid feud you two have going on?"

"Yes," Mason growled. "He has always been deliberately vague about why he has always wanted everything my dad had."

"He didn't tell me anything much, either." Elsa mused, "Well, except…"

"Except what?" Mason frowned.

"That he was the one who paid for your mother's university and bought her an apartment when she was younger and decided to come to Kingston for school."

Mason sat back in his chair. "Really now?"

"Yes!" Elsa nodded, "I told you Toddy was not bad. You should eat. This is really sumptuous."

The food was excellent. As usual, Dotty had outdone herself, but he was troubled.

"My mother never mentioned anything about that."

"She told him not to tell you anything," Elsa said. "Maybe you should talk to her about it."

"I have tried," Mason said, "but she clams up and gets all sad and mopey. When Toddy's name is mentioned she acts like I am trying to destroy her."

"Some people will go to their graves with their secrets," Elsa said contemplatively. "You should talk about the old days and how the business began and find out how your parents met."

"I know how they met." Mason grimaced. "It was at an industry mixer. She was working for the social section of the Sunday News, and she approached my dad for an interview.

My dad said it was instant, the connection he felt to my mom. I understand exactly what he meant."

Elsa looked at him sharply. You do?

"Yep." Mason nodded. "Unfortunately, I do, that kind of connection is pretty rare. It transcends the physical, it's more profound than basic lust. It's a certainty that she is the one. A certainty that is concretized over time. You will do anything for her."

"Like the song that's playing now," Elsa whispered. "You love somebody like that?"

"Yes." Mason nodded.

"Is it Anna Kay?" Elsa widened her eyes. "You still love her?"

"No." Mason snorted derisively. "Anna Kay has been hanging out with Toddy."

"Ewww." Elsa made a face. "Toddy could be her grandfather."

"I want the girl that I love to love me back in the same way. It can't be one-sided. It has to be shared. If not, the relationship will be hell. I think for my dad it was one-sided. Maybe if he didn't die, he and my mom wouldn't have made it."

Elsa nodded. "So who is she, this girl you would do anything for?"

Mason narrowed his eyes and looked at her assessingly. "I don't talk about her with anyone."

"Is it Iris?" Elsa asked casually. "Callie said you two had a special bond."

"Iris?" Mason raised an eyebrow, "your assistant?"

"Yep." Elsa nodded. "I heard she is unfirable."

Mason chuckled. "No, it's not Iris. Callie is way off base. I hired Iris as a personal favor to Trey. He is friends with her sister. Iris turned out to be quite a find, isn't she?"

"Yes," Elsa fiddled with her fork. "She is good at her job."

Mason spared a piece of his fish. It was done in a delicious sauce. He couldn't pinpoint what the flavors were. When he looked up, Elsa had stopped eating and was glaring at him.

"So are you going to tell me who your great love is? The one who you will do anything for?"

Mason smiled. "Why does it matter to you so much?"

"I don't know." Elsa widened her eyes and then looked down at her plate. "Maybe I am a little jealous."

"Say that again," Mason whispered.

"If I loved somebody the way you say you love this person. I wouldn't waste any time with hiding it. Life is too short."

Mason looked at her contemplatively, the curve of her lips, the delicate fan of her eyelashes. She had his heart in a vise, and she didn't even know it. There was no use denying it. He had given Elsa more than a passing thought through the years. It galled him to think about how he used to track her every move. How he felt relief when one of her brief flings or relationships or whatever she called it ended.

"So, you are saying I am wasting time not telling her?" He said out loud. "I don't know about that, my fantasy girl is quite fickle. I am almost sure that being with her will hurt more than being without her. She is still immature in her views of relationships, and I wouldn't want us to get together and then break up. I am not sure how I would handle that."

"She would be stupid to hurt you," Elsa said faintly. "Any woman would be blessed to have a man feel that way about her."

The silence between them mounted. Mason wondered if he could tell her how he felt, but before he could articulate anything, she got up abruptly.

"I need to use the restroom."

"Okay." Mason leaned back in his chair and watched as

she fled. He would give a million dollars now to find out what she was thinking.

Chapter Thirteen

Mason loved someone. Someone he would do anything for. The thought dogged her for the entire weekend. She felt equal parts jealous and then sorrowful. At the back of her mind she had hoped that he felt something for her.

After all, she was the one who had driven him crazy as he had said. And when he said he didn't want her to be his friend. She had seen the look in his eye. His look clearly had said he wanted her otherwise.

But all of that was just lust. Lust was easy, loving someone was a whole other ball game. Love was like that Dennis Brown song that he had playing on loop Thursday night. For you, there is nothing I wouldn't do.

To genuinely mean that for anybody was pretty amazing. Love was selfless. Lust was selfish. She wanted to be the one in the love column, not the lust one. And she wanted to be in the love column for Mason Magnus.

She wouldn't dare admit it out loud. Besides, she was too

late. He had someone else in that column. She imagined who it could be and practically drove herself crazy, trying to come up with the name of Mason's fantasy girl.

Danica visited her on Saturday night, which was a relief from her relentless Mason thoughts. She needed a break from constantly thinking about Mason. What was wrong with her?

She was thinking more about him than she had at any other time in her life, and that included when she was younger, and he was indifferent to her.

Maybe she was one of those people that was turned on by indifference. Mason said he loved another woman, and suddenly she wanted to be the one he loved.

It was like back in the days when he didn't show her any discernible expression at all. She had tried every trick in the book to get a rise out of him.

She had a secret desire to be the center of Mason Magnus' universe. It was that simple and yet that complicated. Toddy texted her in the middle of her feverish thoughts. I want to see you come over for Sunday dinner.

She groaned. He had not brought up the mad idea that he was going to use her in his political tennis match with Mason since his stint in the hospital. And she had not reminded him about it. Now the reprieve was over just when Danica walked through the door with a small travel bag. It was a good distraction. She had something else to think about.

"Hey, you," Elsa greeted her with a hug. She was genuinely happy to see Danica though she had known her for just two and a half years since Giselle discovered her in Florida, and even more miraculously that they were related. Elsa felt close to her as if they had known each other for life.

Danica had that effect on people. She had a sparkly personality, and she was sweet but not overpoweringly so. She was the only child of indulgent parents, and yet she was miraculously unspoiled.

She was also quite pretty, olive-toned golden skin, hazel eyes, and wavy brown hair that she wore in a long high ponytail.

"Why do you have only one travel bag?" Elsa raised an eyebrow. "I thought you were staying here for a while."

"About that," Danica made a face. "I am staying at Guy's townhouse. I just left my things there."

"But why?" Elsa pouted. "I was looking forward to the company."

"I know," Danica sighed, "but I'd be in Tiana's room. If she comes back for a weekend or so I'd displace her, and Guy's townhouse is hardly used, and you won't even be around next week!"

"Mmmm," Elsa made a face. "That's true."

"And yes, I am planning to stay here for a while." Danica grinned. "I am going to find our grandmother, and I am going to eventually meet my online pal. I met him on Christian Singles. He is from here. He says he lives in Kingston. I can't wait."

"You met a guy online? On a dating site?" Elsa frowned at her cousin. "Why?"

"Because I was lonely," Danica said sheepishly. "Good Christian men are slim pickings these days. My pastor recommended it, that is where he met his wife. It is legit."

"Really, now?" Elsa asked skeptically.

"Yes, it is," Danica said defensively. "We don't have pictures of each other either. It cuts down on the lust for your looks angle. We just talk. We moved from emails to texting. I have been talking to him every day for the past year. He has become a huge part of my life. He is so much fun, and to be honest, I am slightly addicted, and I want to meet him."

"You are sure it is a he?" Elsa raised her eyebrow.

"Yup." Danica nodded. "Each applicant is vetted; you can only get on by referral."

"What do you two even talk about?"

"Our lives, our struggles, everything." Danica shrugged. "It's surprisingly easy to do so when you don't have pictures of the other person, and you feel as if you connect on a level that is not superficial."

"I see," Elsa grimaced. "No pictures, I smell a rat, but I am cynical. What's his name?"

"We use aliases. I am Dani, and he is DJ. He wanted to tell me his name some time ago, but I wanted to hold on to the fantasy a little longer. If I knew his name, I would go searching about him on the Internet. I like the anonymity that not knowing gives me. This is going to sound weird, but this is the longest, uncomplicated relationship I have ever had."

"Maybe you should keep it that way," Elsa mused.

Danica sank down in the settee, putting her bag beside her. "Yes, that has crossed my mind, but I think it's time I meet him. I've been yearning to. I want to talk to him face to face, see him laugh instead of an emoji."

"Prepare yourself for disappointment," Elsa said, "be realistic. A man who has to sign up for a dating service no matter if it is Christian or not is probably not that attractive or has some kind of impediment that he feels he has to hide behind a keyboard. What kind of work does he do?"

"He says he is in the medical field," Danica murmured. "I think he was deliberately vague."

"In the medical field, like probably say pharmaceuticals, drugs…" Elsa snorted. "I hope you were just as vague too about key details about yourself."

"Well," Danica worried her bottom lip. "I might have blabbed a few things."

Elsa shook her head disapprovingly.

"I know, I know," Danica said contritely. "It's nothing too personal. I told him I was searching for my grandmother. I told him the whole story how my mother was adopted, and then I met my cousin and found out that my mom had siblings."

"I told him that I was sorry that I didn't get to meet two of my aunts who were killed years ago, but I discovered I had some lovely cousins. I didn't call names."

"Good." Elsa exhaled raggedly. "I don't want some smart cookie piecing together your story, and anything lead back to me. By the way, Tiana and Giselle think you are wasting your time searching for our grandmother."

"My text pal doesn't think so," Danica said. "He is all about knowing who your real family is."

Elsa chuckled. "Of course, he would say that. He will tell you anything to encourage you to feel good about him. I don't trust whoever this is. They are hiding behind a keyboard because they are afraid to meet real people in real life."

"I am glad I am only spending the night with you," Danica said grumpily. "You are so negative."

"And you are too innocent to the ways of the world." Elsa frowned. "Everything is not all joy and light. Maybe you should come with me up to Gordon Town for the week. I could ask my boss. I'll be staying at his house."

"You are trying to protect me." Danica got up and stretched. "Trust me, Elsa, I don't need protecting, I go on vacations alone to faraway places."

"Like where?" Elsa watched Danica.

"Johannesburg, Port Moresby, Brisbane, Beijing, Mumbai, Anchorage..."

Elsa chuckled. "Well, okay then Miss Well-Travelled. I thought you would have named places off the beaten track. I still want to know when you are going to meet your pen pal. I don't want anything to happen to you when you are here on my side of the world."

Danica nodded. "Okay, I will let you know. Enough about me, tell me about your boss, Mason."

Elsa scowled. "There is nothing to tell. "

"Oh come on," Danica grinned, "Giselle said he had a thing for you when you were younger and that he hates your brother, Toddy. There is a story there. Please, please tell me."

Elsa looked at her watch. "Toddy invited us to dinner at his place, we should go."

Danica chuckled. "You will tell me eventually. By the way, I have my résumé all printed and ready for Golden Acres. I am ready to be the next entertainment director. On our way to Toddy's, tell me more about it."

Elsa smiled. "Danica's optimism was infectious. I think you'll do great there. One thing's for sure, they are going to love your sunny personality. Oh, and I have a theory about a lady there named Florence Jackson, I think she is related to our grandmother. I texted aunt Sharla to confirm, and she said that our grandmother's name was Ivy Baxter."

"Oh," Danica clapped her hands in glee. "Yes! A lead!"

"You should hear the story that she wrote," Elsa shook her head, "it was quite disturbing."

"I want to hear it."

"I'll ask Florence for a copy."

Chapter Fourteen

"I like Danica." Myrna declared when Elsa entered the much scaled-down kitchen of Toddy's townhouse.

Elsa was helping her to load the dishwasher. "She's cool."

"Giselle said God brought her into your lives." Myrna mused. "After meeting her today, I am sure of it. She has Toddy promising to give his heart wholeheartedly to Jesus."

Elsa chuckled. "Toddy is a politician and a charmer. He will say and do anything for likes."

Myrna grimaced. "You are right."

She leaned back on the counter as Elsa stacked the dishwasher. "I wish he would slow down, quit politics and all of his other business interests. You know he is taking visitors, holding court in the living room, even when he was wearing his oxygen mask."

"I suspected he'd do that," Elsa said dryly. "At dinner, he said he would only slow down when he is dead."

"Mmmph, he has the ex-wives over here almost on a daily

schedule fawning over him like lovesick fools." Myrna played with the chunky white pearls around her neck. She was still in her church clothes—a white dress with some lace inserts. She had removed her two-toned white shoes and matching bag. Myrna always dressed like a fashion plate when she went to church. I overheard him talking to Celine. He asked her to tell Mason the truth, and she was refusing.

"What truth?" Elsa asked interestedly.

"Keep your voice down," Myrna muttered. "Toddy should tell you this himself. I also heard them arguing about his little manipulative plot to get Mason to back off, by offering you to him. He claims it is his last resort if Celine doesn't come clean. It is wild. I still can't believe you would agree to such a thing."

"He was dying, or so I thought," Elsa finished loading the dishwasher and sat on the barstool at the island. "You should see him in the hospital bed, barely able to breathe. He didn't look like himself, and he made me promise I would help him. How much I can help him is questionable because Mason told me he is in love with someone. Why Toddy thinks Mason would just up and marry me and forget years of careful planning and revenge is beyond me."

Myrna widened her eyes. "Mason is in love?

"Yup." Elsa nodded, "but he won't say with whom."

Myrna laughed. "This is ironic."

She poured herself a glass of carrot juice, the typical Sunday drink from her childhood, but it was no innocent carrot drink. It was laced with Bailey's rum cream. Myrna usually served it in shot glasses.

She was guzzling it down now from a cup. It had to be bad for Myrna to be guzzling down the liquor in her church attire. Her church, in particular, frowned on members having liquor. Myrna usually made a nod to that rule by only drinking liquor in the week and never in her church clothes.

Elsa usually found it funny, but not now. Myrna was the repository of all the juicy news and happenings in Toddy's life and even Mason and Celine's. She worked with Toddy for thirty-six years, she knew all the wives, the girlfriends, and the stories, and she was notoriously tight-lipped about confidential information. Myrna operated on a need to know basis. If you didn't need to know, she was not going to tell you.

"You know who Mason is in love with," Elsa said accusingly.

"I am speculating, but I have a strong hunch." Myrna laughed again, downing another glass of her carrot juice.

"Who is it?" Elsa asked.

"I don't want to assume anything and give you the wrong name. As I said I can only speculate, and if it is who I think it is," Myrna chuckled, "then this is too funny. Toddy's plotting now makes a little sense."

Elsa frowned at her. "You are never this cryptic. Maybe if you tell me what Celine doesn't want Mason to know I could tell him myself and then get him to back off Toddy without the marriage offer and the inevitable rejection of the offer. We all know Mason is not going to give up his revenge to marry me."

"I can't tell you about Toddy and Celine," Myrna shrugged, "I am just the housekeeper. I'll get fired if I blab."

"He'll never fire you," Elsa muttered, "you know that, and you have had more clout with Toddy than any other wife except maybe for Aunt Celine."

Myrna smiled. "These days he and Celine are as thick as thieves. I think they are probably going to get back together."

Elsa narrowed her eyes. "Does Mason know?"

"I don't have a clue." Myrna poured another glass of the

carrot drink. "I haven't spoken to Mason for a month now. I didn't even know he was going to hire you. He always said he couldn't work with you because of his…your… past history." Myrna corrected herself quickly.

"How is he as a boss?"

"He is good." Elsa looked down at the marble countertop. "He said we should forget the past and pretend as if we just met."

"And how is that working out?" Myrna guzzled down another glass of the drink.

"We have lapses," Elsa groaned. "I can't believe he loves someone else. You know what Tiana said, she said that I subconsciously can't keep a relationship because I am always thinking about Mason, that I had some kind of subconscious crush on him and that's why I treated him so mean."

"You were crushed when he gave Giselle and Tiana gifts and didn't give you one," Myrna chuckled. "You threw a tantrum that no one in this house will never forget. You were even jealous of us talking, and I am older than his mother."

Elsa closed her eyes tightly. "I thought you were talking about me behind my back. I wasn't jealous. You two used to have some heart to heart back in the days."

"Really now," Myrna laughed. "That's not how I remember it. Such a pity that you two didn't have a normal relationship as adults together. Mason is a sweet boy."

"A sweet boy," Elsa whispered. "He is not a boy. He is a man, still silent and watchful and reserved."

"But he had a conversation with you about the girl of his heart, didn't he?" Myrna frowned "That is something; that is him opening up."

"But I didn't want to hear that," Elsa said, exasperated. "I didn't want to know that Mason loved some mystery girl. He should have stayed silent and reserved."

"I think it is progress that he is coming out of his shell." Myrna released her grey sister locks from its confined bun and then twisted and turned her neck.

"I hate it when you keep secrets for other people," Elsa growled.

"If I was a blabbermouth, you would not trust me either." Myrna poured herself some water, "This drink is too strong."

"I'd say." Elsa chuckled. "For a woman who doesn't drink in her church dress, you sure were guzzling it down like water."

"I will do better," Myrna vowed, "baby steps. I have already changed a bunch of my old habits, and I am cooking much cleaner these days. Unfortunately, Toddy is not adjusting well to the changes."

"You have been saying the same thing for years." Elsa closed her eyes. "I wish I knew what was going on with Mason."

"Do you realize that since you met Mason, he has been your favorite topic. Even when you were a brat. Back then, I chalked it up to you being a young girl with a huge crush on an adult, and you didn't know how to handle it. But now, it would be interesting to know how you feel about him."

Elsa jumped up from the stool. "I am going to find Toddy. I have to go; I have a busy week ahead."

Myrna chuckled and let the conversation pass. "Your sister Caroline will be coming to Jamaica at the end of the month. Toddy is throwing a party. Put that on your calendar, bring your significant other."

"I don't have a significant other." Elsa hissed, heading out the door.

Myrna chuckled again. "The month is still young."

****

"What did you two talk about?" Toddy asked when Myrna carried the water he requested. He was reclining in his favorite chair, his conversation with Danica had worn him out.

"Her favorite topic, Mason," Myrna grinned. "I don't think she realizes that she talks about him almost every single time she comes over."

"So, you think I am doing the right thing?" Toddy asked. "I mean, I am not used to playing matchmaker, and I do have a vested interest in this."

"I don't know about doing the right thing, but you are certainly going to force Mason's hand." Myrna nodded. "He is going to have to choose between love and revenge. He loved her enough when she was younger to stay away from her. That girl used to push him to his limits as a man."

Toddy grunted. "I would have banned him from the house if you had told me what she was up to."

"I know, but I trusted Mason. He is trustworthy." Myrna looked across at Toddy. "You should just tell him the truth about you and Celine and his father. You know if you all had just told him the whole sordid tale, he would probably have gotten over it by now. And best of all, you wouldn't have to resort to forcing Elsa to marry him."

"Am I forcing her?" Toddy asked dryly. "I asked her to help me out by marrying Mason, she barely protested. Have you ever known Elsa to do anybody's bidding against her will without a fight?"

"No," Myrna sighed. "Stubborn like a mule and argumentative."

"And isn't this your dream to see her married to a good

man? You always said you despaired that Elsa would make the right decision when it comes to men because of my example."

Myrna nodded. "I know what I said, but this might blow up in our faces. Mason is just as stubborn."

"He hired her, and it didn't take much persuading," Toddy said. "We are just nudging them along in the inevitable right direction."

Myrna nodded. "That's the only reason I am entertaining your shenanigans. Those two need help to get together. Both of them are stubborn and need a shove towards each other. And I also want this pointless revenge he has going against you to stop. I want him to start living and get his heart's desire. His heart's desire is not some stupid vindication against you. His heart's desire is Elsa. I know that boy."

"Right." Toddy nodded. "I agree."

"Only because it suits you," Myrna muttered. "You are such a stereotypical politician."

"That's not fair." Toddy grinned. "Not fair at all."

Chapter Fifteen

Elsa went into the office early on Monday to meet with Iris to plan their itinerary for the week. They had settled on a divide and conquer approach, and they were satisfied with their division of labor when Mason popped his head at her door.

"See me when you are done."

She nodded, staring after him when he was gone, quite forgetting what she had been saying to Iris.

Iris chuckled. "He is fine, isn't he?"

"Who, Mason?" Elsa blushed, "I wasn't ogling him."

"Yes, you were." Iris grinned, "but you are forgiven. You are not alone. I mean, all the ladies in this building have looked after him with their mouths half opened at one time or the other. When I started working with him. I got nervous and jittery, but it all evened out. It will feel normal for you after a while."

"Thanks." Elsa murmured.

"As well as it might not." Iris winked at her as she got up.

Elsa headed for Mason's office, feeling a little jittery as Iris had said and hating herself for it.

Mason looked up at her when she entered, his brown eyes looked rich and sparkling as if he was happy. He seemed to be bubbling with it. "How was your weekend?"

Even his voice sounded happy.

Elsa bit back a frown. She didn't want to be a grump, but she had been thinking about him all weekend almost nonstop, and she was sick of thinking about him and the girl he supposedly loved.

"Good," Elsa said, barely holding back the gruffness in her voice, I spent most of the time thinking about you. She didn't mention the last part out loud. She was not crazy.

"How was yours?"

"Relaxing." Mason mused. "I went to Ace's church, their group sang, and Trey had his preaching debut, it was singles weekend."

"Oh, really? Elsa smiled. "Why didn't anyone invite me? I like to hear the Jackson brothers sing, and I am single."

Mason smiled. "It was good, and I am not just saying that because Trey is my cousin, he preached quite a lovely sermon based on 1 John 4:18. Had me chewing over it all weekend."

"There is no fear in love for perfect love casteth out all fear," Elsa said readily. "Don't look so surprised, I went to church growing up, Myrna used to take us. She also insisted on me reading the Bible but frowned when I read out Songs of Solomon dramatically."

Mason chuckled. "You have always provoked poor Myrna."

"So what about the sermon that was so impactful?" Elsa asked.

"Trey made this one point that I am going to act on. He said perfect love is based on a godly decision. Love is not a feeling; it is an act of your will. You make a decision to love, it is not fickle. It doesn't change according to the weather or life circumstances.

"When the person on the other end of this love realizes that you have made that decision and you are not going to change. They stop fearing the million and one things that people fear in a relationship, and they are free to love you back. They are free to make the same decision to love."

"Like a circle," Elsa whispered and then cleared her throat.

"Yes." Mason nodded. "Like a circle. He added that when you fall upon hard times, when romance seems to be wavering, when the pressures of life gets you down, even then, you will have this special love, the love which conquers all fears."

"Because it is a decision." Elsa nodded. "I get it. Is that how you feel about her, your fantasy girl?"

"Yes," Mason said, "that's exactly how I feel. And I came to some important conclusions after our dinner the other night."

"You did?" Elsa asked. "What?"

"You'll know in time," Mason said cryptically. "For now, this is yours." He handed her a set of keys.

"The keys to your heart?" Elsa asked and then choked out, "I meant hearth as in, home, homestead, where you live."

Mason looked at her intently. "I know what hearth is, Elsa. Yes, these are the keys. Dotty is expecting you; my mother will be there for most of the week, she was pleasantly surprised that you will be there too."

"We can catch up on all the family news," Elsa mused. "I know she'll want to hear all the details about Tiana and James."

Mason nodded. "I won't be around for the next week. I'll be going to our Montego Bay office. I have a mammoth task ahead."

"What?" Elsa leaned forward, interested. She liked it when Mason spoke to her like this.

"Edmond Greyson bought himself a chocolate company. He is putting Edmond Junior in charge of that arm of the business. Junior is notoriously picky and finicky. I am not looking forward to working with him."

"You are good at tact and diplomacy," Elsa grinned. "I wish I could come along and see you schmooze."

"If you weren't on this Golden Acres project I would ask you to come along. Maybe you could be my good luck charm. Heather Greyson obviously knows you although you don't know her."

"I think I do though, I was thinking about it when you asked me a couple weeks ago, but it only just came back to me." Elsa mused. "When we were about eight, we did an ad for a chip company."

"Greyson Industries has a snack arm." Mason's eyes lit up.

"Toddy had said his client's wife, suggested that we do the ad. She even came along for the shoot. Is Mrs. Greyson, an Indian woman?"

"Yes," Mason nodded.

"She was at the shoot." Elsa smiled, "I remember now, she wore the most colorful saris. She was quite taken with us. She asked us a lot of questions about our parents. She had tears in her eyes when I told her that my mother was shot. I think she left the room sobbing. If you see her tell her hello from Elsa Pryce, one of the triplets."

"I may not see her," Mason shrugged, "she is not the most sociable person."

"Is Edmond Junior her son?" Elsa asked.

"No. She is Edmond Seniors' second wife; I don't think they have children together. There is no information on Heather anywhere. We checked because Edmond Senior seems to hold her opinion in high regard. We went researching her so that we could please him. We found nothing except that she works with orphans. That is what she loves."

"Ah," Elsa nodded, "Tell her that orphaned Elsa is working with you now. She may tell her stepson to back off. Toddy had said she wanted to take us at one time. He had to tell her no way."

Mason looked at her contemplatively. "Hopefully it won't come to that. It was tough for you growing up, wasn't it?"

"Not really," Elsa shook her head. "We had Toddy."

Mason grimaced. "Was he a good role model? You know I used to come over and was in the house with you for hours unsupervised we could have gotten up to anything. What if I had no qualms about having sex with a teenager?"

"That wouldn't have happened," Elsa cleared her throat. "We had Myrna."

"Who was paid to manage a nine-bedroom three-story mansion." Mason shook his head. "Half the time Myrna didn't know where you were and what you were up to, and you got up to things. I would know I have been your audience."

"My upbringing was fine. I am not blaming Toddy for anything." Elsa growled. "Why do you want me to blame the only family member that saved us from foster care. We had it better than most people!"

"Materially," Mason said, "but I can see why Heather Greyson wanted to take you home with her. She knows about Toddy's many marriages and divorces and girlfriends."

"That was years ago and moot now," Elsa said, "I am all grown up, and I have diagnosed myself as fine.

Mason nodded and changed the subject. "I will be having dinner with you and my mom tonight. Have a good day."

He gave her a look that pinned her to the chair.

Was she mistaken, or was that have a good day loaded with innuendo?

"You too." She got up awkwardly.

****

Elsa drove at a measured pace up the hills toward Gordon Town. She had made an appointment with Ace Jackson for eleven o'clock. He was her first interviewee. She would ask him questions and splice the answers together when she finished with the interview; it would not look as if it was a sit-down affair.

Maybe they could even conduct the interview in one of the scenic luxury locations. Afterward, she would give Ace, Danica's résumé, and then do a few more interviews with some residents.

It was going to be a long day, but Mason would be at the end of it. He had said that he would stop by.

Unbidden anticipation zinged through Elsa as she thought about him stopping by. It was not unlike the way she used to feel as a teenager.

All Myrna had to say was, Mason is coming by today, and she would be hyped up for the evening. She grudgingly remembered how it was. She had never really outgrown it, had she?

Eight years ago…

"Elsa, go and get dressed Mason is coming over." Myrna appeared at the home theater door. "His mother just told me."

It was a day after her sixteenth birthday.

"I am dressed," Elsa said lazily, she was sprawled out in the spacious room alone catching up on her African soaps.

She was in a tiny skirt, which was barely decent and a red bandeau top, no brassier because she didn't need one. She was still waiting for her breasts to grow like aunt Sharla said they would eventually.

"Just do it." Myrna scowled.

Elsa dragged the throw that was over the settee and covered her legs. "There, is that better. Who says that Mason is coming up here anyway?"

"He always seems to find you." Myrna grimaced. "He probably has a birthday present or something. I have no idea why out of the three of you, you treat him like dirt. Why can't you be nicer to him?"

"He likes the abuse." Elsa giggled.

"One day, Myrna glared at her, you are going to wake up and see what a wonderful person he is, and you are going to regret that you were such a brat."

"I won't ever think so," Elsa quipped. "Besides, Mason doesn't care how I treat him, no matter what I say, he doesn't respond. He is an alien, I tell you.

"Or a candidate for ulcer if there ever was one." Myrna left the theater door opened. "If he gives you a present, say thank you and be nice. You can do it; I had a hand in raising you, and I know I didn't raise a philistine."

"Thanks for the encouragement Myrna," Elsa said lazily.

She closed her eyes briefly and drifted off to sleep. It had been a tiring day at school. She knew Mason wouldn't deliberately come and seek her out, Myrna was overreacting as usual.

She pushed off the throw and hugged it between her legs, leaving one butt cheek exposed.

She didn't know what alerted her that someone was in the room. She opened her eyes and saw Mason standing at the door.

"Happy Birthday Elsa Cara Pryce."

She blinked at him. As usual, he was talking in that level husky voice, and he was staring at her without any discernible expression.

"Thanks." She made no move to cover herself. "Do you want to kiss me for my birthday, Mason?"

She asked in her best seductress voice.

Mason didn't move. "No."

"Liar," Elsa whispered. "Come here, Mason. Come and kiss me. I am at the age of consent; nobody will send you to jail."

There was no change in his expression. He walked further into the room and sat down in a chair opposite hers.

"I thought that this birthday, you would stop acting like this. I had hoped for a sprinkling of maturity."

Elsa chuckled. "Maturity is overrated. I don't want to be serious and buttoned up like you. I want to be a free spirit to love, laugh, and have lots of sex with many different men. I don't want to be a dweeb."

"You mean you want to be burdened with a couple STDs and fatherless kids?" Mason watched her as she stretched seductively. "Don't you ever get tired of the same old tired routine?"

"As a matter of fact, yes. I am tired." Elsa jumped up and winked at him. "I know just the thing to get you to move. I have been thinking about it. When I am done, I am going to get you to stop being a stuck-up pig."

"A stuck-up pig?" He didn't even crack a smile or look outraged.

"Did you get me a present this year Mason Magnus?"

"I did," Mason said. "I got you one last year, too, but decided against giving it to you because you misbehaved. There should be no reward for your behavior."

"All I did was strip for you to the song Private Dancer. You liked it, admit it."

"I want you to stop acting like a teenage nymphomaniac and to be serious for once!" Mason said. "Can you do that?"

"It depends," Elsa pouted. "What did you get me?"

Mason reached in his pocket and removed a jewelry box.

"Ooh, is that an engagement ring?" Elsa walked over and took it from him.

"If we got married you would tire me out by your next birthday, I would be returning you to your brother by the middle of the year," Mason said solemnly. "But I am hoping that one day, you will at least be more mature. I see glimmers of it when you are not performing. Maybe then I will give you an engagement ring."

"I'll always act this way. I'll always be the same. Why do you want to change me?" Elsa pouted and opened the jewelry box. It was a gold chain with her names at the pendant—Elsa Cara.

"Thank you," Elsa whispered. She thought she saw his eyes soften.

"You are welcome, Elsa."

Surely this meant she had won. He felt something.

Elsa grinned triumphantly. "So you do like me, you want me! Admit it."

His eyes turned hard again. "Elsa…"

"I'll make you admit it." Elsa pulled off her top and then her skirt, "I'll make you want me if it's the last thing I do."

She sprawled off in the settee. "Admit it, Mason, you want to ravish me."

She started touching herself and closed her eyes, saying

the lewdest things to him.

He watched her with absolutely no expression on his face. When she opened her eyes again, he was gone.

Chapter Sixteen

After her walk down memory lane, Elsa was feeling a little bit uncomfortable for the rest of the day. She had both managed to arouse and repel herself at the same time. Why had it been so important to her that Mason admit that he wanted her?

She had the interview with Ace, and it was a struggle for her to concentrate on what he said. He didn't comment on her obvious bundling at the beginning of the shoot. It was when she was packing up that he asked, "Everything okay?"

"Yes, sure." Elsa nodded. "I was a bit distracted coming over."

"How is it going with Mason?"

"So you think he is the one that has me distracted? Elsa asked, "why can't it be someone else, something else?"

"Was it something else or someone else?" Ace smiled.

"No," Elsa sighed, "I took a walk down memory lane, remembered how I was when I was younger. I liked Mason back then, but I expressed it in a totally childish and reprehensible way. I don't know if he is ever going to see me differently."

"I think he does see you differently," Ace said, "He is proud of the work you have done so far on our campaign. He told me so himself."

"It is possible that Mason hates me as a person," Elsa whispered. "By the way, I have no evidence to back that up. I just…I was awful. I used to offer myself to him, daring him to have sex with me…"

"You were testing him, his integrity, his patience." Ace frowned. "I sincerely doubt that Mason hates you, Elsa. I think you are over exaggerating."

"You don't know what I did to him." Elsa sighed. "And now Mason has this perfect love that he told me about, and I feel the urge to stand up in front of him and shout, choose me, love me."

"You mean from the sermon that Trey preached?" Ace looked at her contemplatively. "He told you about it?"

"Yup, that's the one." Elsa made a face. "He made up his mind to love some girl perfectly."

Ace chuckled. "You should see your expression when you said that."

Elsa made a face. "I hate her!"

"You should tell Mason how you feel about him." Ace chuckled, "and lay off the hate talk. She could be a very lovely person."

"Nope, never gonna happen." Elsa shook her head, "I can't tell Mason how I feel. I have been rejected by him one too many times."

Ace leaned forward, "Elsa, the secret to appealing to Mason is to appeal to his mind. He is a cerebral person; those kinds of people are not very outwardly emotional. In the past, you thought that he was the stereotypical male, so you threw yourself at him, he doesn't operate like that. You viewed his withdrawal as rejection. Maybe he is more turned on by your intelligence?"

Elsa stared at Ace. "Say what?"

"I know," Ace said ruefully, "it is possible. There are men like that. Not all of us wear our emotions on our sleeves or listen to the dictates of our penis. That doesn't mean though that Mason has no emotions."

"That's all good and well, but he loves someone else, and you and I know that you can't force Mason to do anything. Oh, by the way," Elsa rummaged in her camera bag for Danica's résumé. "Here is my cousin's résumé. She is interested in the entertainment director's job. She is bubbly and sweet and loves older people. A perfect fit for the job. You should see her last night, completely had Toddy eating out of her palms."

Ace nodded. "Okay, I'll pass this on to Lily. She will call her for an interview."

"Thank you." Elsa beamed. "Sorry, I can't chat some more; you are a good listener."

"So I've been told." Ace said ruefully. "It was nice chatting with you too. You should do more of that with Mason."

Elsa made a face. "No more Mason talk, I have another interview."

****

Her next interview was with Florence Jackson, Tobias' widow. She had been anticipating speaking to her since she read her story, Nine o'clock, the one that mentioned her sister Ivy and she wanted to know more.

Florence was delighted to see her.

Florence lived in one of the original bungalows. Hers was a three-bedroom, and she had a delightful little garden in front of it.

"I do my own gardening," She led Elsa to the back patio where she had a fragrant herb garden. Her lavender plants were blossoming. She had a giant potted one on her veranda.

"I distill them and make my own essential oil," Florence sat with her back to her lavender plant, while Elsa set up the camera.

"I haven't done much since Tobias died, I lost interest."

"You two never had children together?" Elsa asked.

"We had a son who died in his early thirties." Florence sighed. "He was a decorated soldier in the US Army, fought in a couple of wars and was injured got hooked on drugs. He died of an overdose."

"I am so sorry," Elsa murmured.

"It was heartbreaking at the time, but time has a way of dulling the pain," Florence said philosophically. "I had a long interesting life; it wasn't pain-free."

"Tell me about that." Elsa turned to her. "Your story about your childhood was fascinating. Did you ever use that knife under your pillow?"

"No." Florence grimaced. "My mother did."

"Oh," Elsa widened her eyes.

"She caught him in my room." Florence snorted. "She couldn't deny what I was telling her anymore, she was not happy with what I saw."

"Did she go to jail?" Elsa asked.

"No, she didn't kill him, just stabbed him in the legs." Florence sighed. "We fled the community together after that and left everything we had behind, which wasn't much mind you. We wanted to go for my sister Ivy, but she was heavily pregnant and was already given to a son of my father's friend as a wife. He sold her. Actually, the friend owed him money, and he wanted to get the daughter he had impregnated off his hands.

"Ivy was just fourteen at the time. My mother always vowed to go back for Ivy, but she never did. We couldn't afford to for years. We fled to some family members of hers in the town. We then moved to the Western side of the island when my mother got a job as a practical nurse.

"We had it rough for a long while. When I was around twelve, my father died. At fourteen, my mother died from the flu and I became a ward of the State. I met Tobias Jackson when I was a young nurse, he was a widower and an older gentleman, but he treated me right."

"Wow," Elsa was speechless. "So much tragedy in your life. What happened to Ivy?"

"I lost track of her." Tears came to Florence's eyes, and she wiped them away. "My one regret was that I never saw my sister again. She would protect me from him, you know. She always put up a fight with that man."

"Was your maiden name Baxter?" Elsa asked, tensing up herself for the answer.

"Yes," Florence nodded. "How did you know? I never use it. I couldn't wait to purge it from my records. When I married Tobias, I took the name Jackson so fast, you would have gotten whiplash. I didn't want that man's name tainting me. He was a sick son of a…, is the camera still rolling?"

"Yes," Elsa chuckled, and then she sobered up, "you know my grandmother's name was Ivy Baxter Kennedy."

Florence sat forward in her chair. "Really?"

"Yes," Elsa nodded, "she got married to…"

"Winston Kennedy?" Florence gasped, and then she got up and then sat down, shook her head, and then stared at Elsa in awe.

"This is not happening. I am dreaming, aren't I?"

"It is happening," Elsa whispered, feeling stunned herself.

"It's a small world. I have been praying for years for just a glimmer of a word about Ivy. I say to God every night, please be with Ivy God. Look out for her.

"Listen, I looked, and I looked, and I couldn't find her anywhere, and yet here you are a granddaughter. Tell me everything," Florence continued talking without pause. "Is she okay? She would be in her late sixties now. She is still as pretty, isn't she? She was a beautiful girl and bright with so much potential.

"I am sure she made something of herself, triumphed against our childhood if anyone could do that, Ivy could. She was a fighter. She never made it easy for our father to rape her, and he couldn't touch me if she was around. He was actually afraid of her though she looked slight. She was the one who told me to keep a knife under my pillow."

"I don't know anything about her," Elsa said faintly. "She left Winston and her children behind, and never looked back."

"Oh goodness," Florence muttered, "abandoned by her own, she turned around and did the same?"

"Yes," Elsa sighed. "Our family history was not pretty either, after she abandoned her three girls. My mother was the oldest, and she took care of her sisters, Hannah and Sharla. We discovered that she had another child, Sara, when she left and put her up for adoption. We just discovered Sara the other day. Her daughter Danica applied for a job up here too."

Florence nodded sadly. "I will see that Danica gets the job. I looked for Ivy everywhere. Tobias, and I even hired a detective, had the man scouring all of Portland."

"Maybe she wasn't there. She left when my mother was

fifteen." Elsa glanced back at the camera to ensure that it was still recording. She would have to send the unedited video to her sisters and Danica and the Wileys.

"This is bittersweet," Florence said sadly. "I wish your grandmother was around. It would be nice to hug her again. She had a good heart. I am telling you; I don't understand how she could leave her children behind. She was so protective of me."

"I have no clue either." Elsa shook her head.

"How did your mother take the abandonment?" Florence wiped away tears again. "I feel so bad now, I have nieces, and I didn't know it. I had a family; I could have helped you all."

"Don't feel bad, Florence," Elsa said sympathetically, "you don't sound as if you had an easy time of it in your youth either."

"I bet your mother was a good mother; you seem like a lovely well-adjusted young lady." Florence sniffed. "I would love to meet her."

"I didn't grow up with her, and I am not sure how well adjusted I am." Elsa cleared her throat. "Our aunt Hannah, the sister that followed her, got involved with a married man. She was a hairdresser and worked from home. One day, her boyfriend's wife stopped by and shot Hannah, my mother, her husband, and herself. To this day it's still known as the Drapers Massacre."

"I remember Jennifer Riddley Wiley." Florence made the sign of the cross. "I heard the news at the time while I was in New York. I cried when I heard, and I had no idea why. It's not as if bad news didn't come from Jamaica, but that news touched something within me."

"Maybe it was because you had six orphaned grand nieces and nephews if you but knew it." Elsa sighed. "My father died before I was born, so my sisters and I had no one. Hannah had three sons too. Aunt Sharla was the only one left, and she had just migrated to Canada."

"Goodness." Florence made a moaning sound." I wonder if our family is cursed?"

"Maybe our generation broke the curse?" Elsa said hopefully. "We started off shaky but ended up okay. The six orphaned Wiley boys lived together; a cousin was their guardian. He robbed them blind and they almost lost everything again. As for us, we were taken in by our brother, Toddy Pryce."

"God bless him," Florence said with heartfelt force. "He took in three baby girls. He deserves all the blessings of heaven."

"Yes," Elsa nodded, "and we were all at the same age. We are triplets."

"A prince among men." Florence praised Toddy again.

"I think so." Elsa sighed. "Toddy is many things, but he is all about family. That's why I would do anything for him."

She thought about his proposal that she be offered to Mason and realized that it was a simple ask. She loved Mason anyway. She wouldn't mind marrying him either. It was a rare bout of honesty for her, and the thought stunned her into silence.

Florence didn't seem inclined to talk either. She was absorbing the information that Elsa had unloaded on her.

"I want to find your grandmother," She finally said with tears in her eyes.

"You will have a search partner in Danica, it is her desire that she finds Ivy too," Elsa said absently. "Tell me about the amenities here and how you feel living here."

Florence was not much use to her after that. She was more interested in the children. She wanted to meet everyone;

she was anxious that they were okay. She wanted to hear everybody's story. They took a break for lunch, and they spoke until Elsa's camera battery died, and the evening shadows crept up on them.

Chapter Seventeen

Elsa arrived at Mason's place and followed the music to the kitchen. Celine was singing Des'Ree Gotta Be at the top of her voice. Listen as your day unfolds, Challenge what the future holds, try to keep your head up to the sky, Lovers, they may cause you tears, Go ahead, release your fears, Stand up and be counted, Don't be ashamed to cry

She hugged Elsa and kissed her on both cheeks and continued singing.

Something amazing smelling was sizzling in the several pots on the stove.

"Where should I put my bag?" Elsa asked loudly. She could barely hear herself as Celine danced around the kitchen.

"This way, Miss Elsa," Dotty tapped her on the shoulder. "Sorry, I didn't hear you come in!"

"That's understandable," Elsa shouted when they headed up the stairs.

"When she gets this way, she turns the music up and dances

her way through several dishes. I am amazed that they come out so well."

Elsa giggled. "I know. I lived with her for three years."

"Oh," Dotty looked at her, "so you know Mr. Mason a long time then?"

"Ten years." Elsa nodded. "Celine was married to my brother."

Dotty showed her to a spacious room that was finished with earth-toned colors and green details. "I like this!" Elsa said, looking around.

"Please enjoy your stay, Miss Elsa." Dotty left her to her own devices. The first thing she did was call Danica.

I gave your résumé to Ace Jackson. He is one of the owners at Golden Acres," Elsa said, "and you won't believe this."

"What?" Danica asked.

"Remember Florence Jackson, that I was telling you about? I am almost 99.9% sure she is our grandmother's sister. She is the widow of the man who owned Golden Acres. It's a coincidence."

"Yes," Danica whispered, "it's a miracle. I prayed about this!"

Elsa resisted the urge to roll her eyes. She didn't know if God listened to little prayers like this.

"Well, then God heard your prayers," she said out loud to Danica. "I recorded my conversation with Florence so you, Giselle, Tiana, Jordan, Guy, and Case can hear. I found you people a grand-aunt. I will send the video to all of you in the family group."

"Yes!" Danica chirped, "I can't wait! Does she know where our grandmother is?"

"No," Elsa sighed, "it's a long story, and I said I recorded it so that you can hear. I have to go and get ready for dinner; Celine is cooking up a storm."

"Yes, well, I am going to Jordan's house for dinner," Danica giggled, "I have a packed calendar of social events for the rest of the week too. I'll be at Walter and Aisha's place tomorrow evening, Giselle and Pete are taking me out Thursday night. I am spending Saturday night with Saint and Sandrene. Then I spend Sunday with Preston and Sheryl, and then to top it all off, next weekend, I am going to a Case Wiley concert in Grand Cayman. Lyla is coming to pick me up. We'll be spending time at Preston's villa."

"So when are you going to work, if you get the job?" Elsa asked, "and it is a guarantee you will get it. Florence said she would make sure you did."

"I know," Danica said apologetically, "most of these outings are in the evenings and on the weekend. I will be available for work whenever I get the call."

"Okay," Elsa grunted. "I feel a wee bit jealous of you and these outings."

"Don't be," Danica laughed, "you have had them all for most of your life, you all have a history together and memories. I am the shiny newcomer; everybody will soon get tired of me."

"Yep, that's true." Elsa murmured. "I am just a cow."

Danica laughed. "You know I heard the skepticism in your voice when I said I prayed about getting a break in finding our grandmother, but see, it happened."

"Does God answer prayers like that, though?" Elsa asked. "I mean, do you really think me coming up here and hearing Florence's story and then finding out more about her life was God's doing or just a fortunate coincidence. I would have heard her anyway, whether you prayed about it or not. I would have put two and two together anyway. I would have known she was my aunt anyway, and without prayer."

"I like to think of it like this," Danica said contemplatively,

"I believe there is a God, and that he is our maker and that he is interested in our affairs. I also believe that specific circumstances are adjusted by him to benefit us when we ask him to intervene. And I believe he does intervene."

Elsa snorted. "I am still a skeptic."

"You should try it out," Danica said. "Ask him to work out the situation with you and Mason and then watch what happens."

"There is no situation with me and Mason," Elsa said. "He wants revenge against Toddy. There is no way he is going to choose me over that. Besides, he loves someone else. I am not in the running. He has perfect love for this woman, and he has decided that he will love her forever. God is not going to change that. Mason made up his mind!"

"Just do it," Danica said, "I dare you."

Elsa made a face at the phone when Danica hung up but a little part of her where the skepticism hadn't taken over yet, forced her to close her eyes and pray, God if you rearrange stuff because we ask, please work out the situation with Mason and Toddy. Please help Mason to let go of his revenge.

She opened her eyes, feeling self-conscious. She hadn't asked about her and Mason. Obviously, that was not happening with Mason and the fantasy girl he had perfect love for.

A quick shower later and a change of clothes, and she joined Celine downstairs.

****

"Sorry about the loud music earlier," Celine grinned, "I was caught up in the moment."

"I remember that music is a part of your cooking process." Elsa smiled. "You were missed when you left.

"I miss you girls so much," Celine came over and hugged her again. "You get prettier every time I see you."

"Thanks, Celine." Elsa grinned, "and you look like you haven't aged a day."

"I think I aged a thousand years the last week when I heard that Toddy was in the hospital," Celine frowned, "I obviously have a lingering affection for him."

"Obviously, Myrna says the two of you may get back together." Elsa cleared her throat.

"Oh, I love Toddy, but I am not an idiot." Celine chuckled. "He is near and dear to me but very predictable."

"So how do you manage when Mason tells you about his plans for Toddy?" Elsa asked.

"Mason doesn't tell me anything about that, and I like to pretend that it is not happening." Celine headed to the stove. "I cooked up a storm, I have meat and vegetarian options and fish, and I baked, but I know that you don't have a sweet tooth."

"Never did." Elsa grinned.

"Tiana was the only one of the three of you who appreciated my baking," Celine grinned, "Giselle was too busy with training, and you think sugar is a drug. Do you still think so?"

Elsa nodded. "Yep, I still think so."

"You are refreshingly the same." Celine looked at the clock. "How are your sisters getting on? Update me while I make a sauce, Mason should be here shortly. I would like us to eat together."

"Tiana is getting married in December, and she got a job as a producer on the show she helped write. Giselle is graduating next year with her master's degree. Took her a while, she stopped a couple of times."

Celine nodded. "I know all of that, which means I am in

the loop."

"You are in the loop," Elsa repeated. "And there is something new. I just found out I have a grand aunt. Well, I am speculating, but it is a strong possibility."

"Really?" Celine widened her eyes. "One more family member. Tell me more."

"It's an amazing coincidence." Elsa began telling her, Celine listened attentively and then shook her head amazement. "You'll have to repeat this for Mason. He is interested in these kinds of things."

"He doesn't strike me as the family man type," Elsa wrinkled her nose.

"Oh, he is." Celine murmured. "Why do you think there is a feud between Mason and Toddy? Mason is defending his father's legacy."

"Yes, there is that." Elsa nodded.

"Now tell me about you," Celine pointed at her. "I hear about Tiana and Giselle, but you are the dark horse in all of this, are you dating anyone?"

"Nope." Elsa shrugged. "I am happily single."

"Happily?" Celine raised an eyebrow. "Are you telling me the truth, Elsa?"

"Semi happily," Elsa shrugged. "I am not sad or looking for anyone."

"You sound like Mason," Celine mused. "He had a ghastly girlfriend last year, a smug little madam named Chandra. She was a botanist. We rarely met because Mason doesn't introduce me to his dates, but the few times I was around her, I prayed for his deliverance. She actually told me and Celia that we didn't know anything about flowers. She called us novices to our faces. We were gardening long before that girl was even born."

"How dare her?" Elsa chuckled. "Maybe she is the girl that

he loves."

"No, never." Celine shook her head. "I know my boy, and she is not his type."

"What is Mason's type?" Elsa asked curiously.

Celine smiled. "I can recall you asking me that as a teenager."

"And you never did answer," Elsa smirked. "Because he is so secretive, and you really don't know."

"I do know," Celine said mysteriously.

"You are just as secretive as he is," Elsa accused, "Toddy told me that he knew your family from Portland and that you all were close."

"What else did he tell you?" Celine looked at her, an uneasy look on her face.

"Nothing." Elsa shrugged, "but it doesn't exactly seem like top secret information."

"I'd rather not talk about the early days," Celine said softly. "It's all in the past."

"But maybe if you told Mason what really went down between you and Toddy and his father, he wouldn't be pursuing this revenge plot against Toddy, and I would not be a pawn in it."

"You are not a pawn," Celine fanned her off. "You don't have to agree to whatever Toddy is planning. You are a grown woman with no obligation to your brother. He did the right thing in taking you and your sisters in when you were orphaned, and knowing Toddy, he does not expect anything in return. You want to be a pawn, and there lay the difference."

"So you do know about it." Elsa breathed.

Celine nodded. "I do. For the record, I told Toddy it was ridiculous."

Elsa snorted. "You should all just be honest with Mason

and stop this!"

"Let's talk about honesty," Celine looked at Elsa knowingly. "You do realize that you are not fooling anyone, if Mason stops his vendetta against Toddy because of you, it would be your dream come true. You've been pursuing Mason since you were a little girl!"

"I wasn't!" Elsa gasped. "That's not true."

"I was there, I saw the way you looked at him," Celine said dryly. "You should just tell him that you love him and you both deal with this, instead of having Toddy do your dirty work for you. I know you are afraid of rejection, and that is why you use insults and whatever it is you hide behind."

"None of this is true," Elsa murmured, all the steam escaping her.

"Why do you keep your hair short?" Celine asked.

"Because I like it," Elsa looked at Celine like she had lost her mind.

"Wasn't it because Mason said it looked good on you? I was there, remember. He saw a picture of Halle Berry in one of the magazines you were leafing through and he said, Elsa, that hairstyle would look great on you. The next day you chopped off your tailbone length hair and you haven't grown it back since."

"No!" Elsa growled, "this is ridiculous."

"And you are in denial." Celine looked pleased, "bad denial."

"What is Elsa in denial about?" Mason appeared at the doorway, he looked between his mother and her.

"The reason why she cut her hair." Celine smiled at him beatifically. "I didn't hear you come in."

"I stopped and was talking to Rufus about the grapes he planted alongside the house. Good evening to both of you."

Elsa nodded at him shyly. She felt as if she were seeing

him for the first time. As usual, his presence filled up the space.

She looked at him helplessly. Her observations didn't matter. He had perfect love for some perfect girl.

He looked at her quizzically. "What's going on, Elsa. You seem different."

"Nothing is going on," Elsa looked away from him and then into Celine's knowing eyes.

"Your mother is keeping secrets from you."

Mason turned to his mother. "Mom?"

"Elsa is the one keeping secrets." Celine threw the ball right back in her court. "Why don't you tell him how you used to ask me a million and one questions about what his favorite colors were and what made him tick."

Mason turned back to her and smiled, "Is that so?"

"I was building a psychological profile." Elsa cleared her throat. "I wanted to know if you were human."

Mason laughed indulgently, and then the talk turned to general matters. But all of a sudden, Elsa felt so aware of Mason that while they were at dinner and he passed the salt, his fingers brushed hers and she felt a zap of electricity.

She looked at him, shocked, and Mason raised an eyebrow. "You felt that?"

"Yes, I did." Elsa nodded.

"Strike sparks off each other, huh," Celine said smugly. "I always knew this would happen."

"Nothing is happening," Elsa said stubbornly.

Chapter Eighteen

Elsa had asked the question aloud to Tiana a week and a half later. "What exactly is happening to me?"

"The dam has broken; that's what," Tiana said in her ear. "You have stopped lying to yourself, and now you are a woman living her truth."

"Living my truth?" Elsa murmured. "And what's my truth?"

"That you have it bad for Mason." Tiana cackled. "You want to marry him and have his babies."

"You have stars in your eyes because you are happy with James, not everyone wants to get married and have babies." Elsa grumbled, "I called to tell you that I did your invitations. I sent it via email for your approval."

"Thank you," Tiana sounded like she was settling down for a long conversation, and Elsa groaned out loud, she still had a load of work to do.

She could hear the cleaning service people in the building.

Tiana ignored her groan. "I will be inviting Florence to my wedding. I finally watched the video in its entirety. I never had the chance to do so until now. Can I get her number, please? I need to talk to her." Tiana sobered up. "That's some story she told you."

"Yep." Elsa murmured.

"So our mom was a child of incest? Monique Pryce was an incestuous baby?" Tiana asked tentatively. "Ivy was pregnant around that time, wasn't she? Pregnant at fourteen for her own father, who sold her to a family friend. Is this real?"

"I didn't want to think about it." Elsa sighed. "I don't want to process that."

"She went through a lot." Tiana mused, "I am not saying she did a good thing in abandoning her children, but I can now understand the motivation."

"And don't forget, she was physically abused." Elsa snarled. "He was a monster."

"Now, I am actually curious about where our grandmother could be." Tiana mused, "I would just give her a hug. No recriminations from my end."

"Me too, actually," Elsa said, "Danica is on it, she and Florence are now acting as detectives. I will hear when they come up with anything."

"So has Toddy asked Mason to choose you or revenge yet?" Tiana asked, jumping to what really interested her.

"Not that I know of," Elsa said, "Toddy is still recovering. I don't think bartering my hand in marriage is on his mind."

Tiana laughed. "Update me when he does offer you on a platter. By the way, Aunt Celine said she is going to feature my wedding in her magazine."

"That's nice, good marketing for your series, the great house, and James," Elsa said. "Now I have to go, I am putting the finishing touches on the ad campaign. I'll have to present it to Mason when he comes back tonight and to the clients tomorrow. Wish me luck."

"You will do great," Tiana said. "Tell Mason hello from me. Tell me something, are you bringing him as your plus one to the wedding or should I give him his own invitation."

"I don't know." Elsa grunted. "I have to go, you are just trying to goad me into something."

She hung up and then glanced at the clock. She had been driving it hard to put together something special for Golden Acres, and she was ahead of schedule too.

For the past week and a half, Mason had been calling to check in on her progress, and now he was finally here waiting to see what she had come up with.

She took a deep breath and headed to his office. She hadn't seen him since the dinner with his mother at his house. He had left the next morning before she had even woken up. Their conversations over the phone had been surprisingly relaxed and friendly. It was a turn for them, they hadn't been able to communicate so effortlessly before and for so long on a wide variety of topics.

She hadn't wanted it to end, but now Mason was back and in his office. Callie had long gone home.

She knocked on the door before she entered.

"Hey," Mason looked up from his computer and smiled. "You are a sight for sore eyes. Give me a minute. I have to fire off an email to Junior Greyson. They are launching a new line of snacks, and they are keeping us as their advertisers."

Elsa nodded and sat down.

"Let's go to dinner," Mason said, looking up, "I am starving. Tomorrow you show me what you have."

He got up.

Elsa got up too. "Where are we going?"

"Gloria's," Mason picked up the phone. "I want a seat on the outside, I have been looking forward to this all week. I'll call ahead."

Elsa smirked. "I bet you weren't thinking of me as your dinner partner."

Mason picked up his cellphone. "As a matter of fact, I was. I like your company. I liked talking to you on the phone these past couple of days."

"Me too." Elsa smiled. "It was different and yet good. I thought you didn't want to be my friend."

"I didn't." Mason gave her a half-smile, flashing his white teeth. "But you have been growing on me."

"I don't know what to say." Elsa fake fanned her face.

"We say nothing." Mason looked at her. "We are going to play this by ear. Whatever happens, happens."

They did get a seat on the deck at the restaurant. It was buzzing with people as usual. Mason was a well-known and well-loved customer. He didn't have to wait.

"You turned out to be my good luck charm," Mason said after they were seated and were served the broth and bread. "I went to the Greyson household for a business lunch, I told Heather Greyson that you said hello and she was so over the moon happy that you remembered her. I ended up talking about you and Tiana and Giselle for most of the time. She peppered me with questions. She wanted to know if you girls grew up all right."

"Really?" Elsa couldn't believe it.

"Yes," Mason nodded. "Junior didn't get a word in edgewise. He left with his father because Heather didn't want me to go. She kept going on and on about you three and the Wiley brothers. I had a warm time extricating myself from that conversation, but..."

"But?" Elsa raised an eyebrow.

"It seemed to make her husband happy that she was so animated. Edmond Senior said that she went through spates of depression lately, and it was nice to see her so upbeat. He told Junior to treat me right."

Elsa laughed. "Did he?"

"He was as calm as a well-fed pussycat. You know if you squint your eyes and look at Junior Greyson in the half-dark he looks like a well fed orange tabby. Sometimes I expect him to flick his wrist and start cleaning himself."

Elsa laughed out loud. "That's funny…Well then, I am happy I could help."

"And you will get the opportunity to help even more. They are having their annual first of January charity ball." Mason looked at her contemplatively. "Heather said she wanted you to help with the promotion, she also said I should bring you as my date."

"Ah… really?" Elsa smiled. "A client has to force you to take me out?"

"I can't be forced to do anything." Mason shrugged. "And trust me, taking you out will be my pleasure."

Elsa blushed. She literally could feel her ears heating up. "Mason…"

"Elsa…" he said just as huskily.

"What's the charity for?" Elsa finally choked out.

"Orphans. They contribute to several homes, and they contribute millions of dollars from the proceeds of the ball to a particular home each year."

"Oh," Elsa nodded. "That's admirable."

"It's black tie event, a really exclusive part of the yearly calendar," Mason said. "You should give Heather a call."

"I will." Elsa shifted in her seat and fidgeted in her chair.

Mason narrowed his eyes on her. "What's wrong?"

"I don't know, I…" her voice trailed away. "I want to

be…I can't do this."

"Do what?" Mason leaned closer to her. "What's wrong, Elsa? Talk to me. I thought we were getting on great over the phone these last couple of days."

"I like you!" Elsa said it a bit too loudly. She looked around but nobody else was paying them any attention. "I probably more than like you and for a very long time."

Mason hadn't shifted after her outburst. He took her hand in his from across the table and laced his fingers with hers.

"I like you too." Mason squeezed her fingers. "I am happy we got that out of the way."

****

It was torture working with Mason Magnus.

That's what it was. She had all but admit her feelings for him, and he had benevolently patted her on the back and said, 'there there I like you too, Elsa.'

He was treating her just like he did when she was a tormented teenager. He hadn't indicated that anything had changed for them. It was business as usual and she resented that.

But what did she really want?

They had finalized the advertising package for Ace and Quade together. They had worked pretty late every night, ironing out all the kinks and incorporating the feedback from Ace. She was sure that he was silently laughing at her. He had caught her more than once looking at him with lost puppy eyes. He was probably laughing up a storm in his office about her obvious fascination with him.

"What's wrong?" Mason said above her head.

Elsa looked up at him blearily. She wanted to tell him that she was conflicted about him, but instead, she said, "I have been missing the gym. I need a workout. I need to get really tired and really sweaty so that I can sleep like a baby."

Mason removed his glasses. "There is a gym at my apartment, you can join me if you want. I usually go after work."

Elsa swallowed. There it was again, that intensity that made her feel as if she couldn't breathe. "I wouldn't want to intrude."

"We'll probably have the gym to ourselves at this hour." He put back on his glasses and glanced at his watch. "It's after eight on a Thursday."

"Do you have your clothes with you?"

"I always have a gym bag in my car. Elsa got up. "So, we are doing this?"

"Yep." Mason nodded. "We are. I'll let the guard know you will be stopping by regularly."

"I have my own gym." Elsa snorted. "I don't need yours."

"My apartment is just three minutes from here," Mason said. "The gym even has a sea view, or if you are up for some competition, we could play tennis. There are four courts. Usually, one is available now."

"I am sold." Elsa grinned. "I am going to beat you good."

****

The apartment gym was obviously new and clean. "I like it here, Elsa looked around. They were alone. A television was on and set to a sports channel.

"I am just going to pop up to my apartment and change and get the rackets," Mason said hesitantly. "You can change through there, unless you want to come with me."

"To your apartment, alone with you?" Elsa whistled. "Aren't you afraid for your virtue."

"When you were younger, I was, but not now. I think I am safe now."

"I will never live that down." Elsa through over her shoulder as she headed for the changing rooms.

"Be back soon," Mason called after her. "You can meet me courtside."

Elsa waited for Mason courtside, as he had suggested. She stretched to get the knots out of her neck.

"Elsa Pryce." It was Ace Jackson. "Why am I not surprised to see you."

Elsa looked at him. "Let me guess, you live here?"

"No," Ace shook his head, "DJ lives here. I occasionally stop by to whip him at tennis."

"DJ?" Elsa frowned.

"My brother, Deuce. He hates the name Deuce, so he has been DJ since he was six. Have you ever met him?"

"Not formally," Elsa said, "I have seen him and heard him sing with you and Trey."

Ace turned to his brother who was texting on the phone. "DJ! Come and meet a real live woman."

"He has an online relationship," Ace chuckled. "I have never seen anything like it. He tells her what he eats, what he's wearing, what he is going to do next and yet he has never met her in person, she could be a he for all we know."

Elsa laughed and then widened her eyes. "Is he on that Christian singles site thing?"

"Yes." Ace raised an eyebrow. "You know about it?"

"Uhuh." Elsa's mind was spinning. Danica said her online buddy was DJ, what if it were this DJ? Deuce Jackson was a doctor, Danica said her DJ was in the medical profession.

"He has been haranguing me to join," Ace made a face. "I have so far resisted."

"My cousin joined it," Elsa said. "She thinks it's great."

Deuce looked up. Elsa did a double-take. "And I thought you were handsome, Ace. Was he always this hunky?"

Ace laughed and introduced them. "Elsa, this is my brother, Deuce Jackson, aka DJ."

Deuce shook her hand. "Hello, Elsa. It's nice to officially meet you, even though I feel as if I know you, since I know Tiana, and you have her face."

Elsa grinned. "I am older than Tiana by two minutes. Actually, she has my face."

"So are we playing doubles? Mason asked behind them, "because I am ready."

"Yes!" Ace jumped at the chance. "I hope you are up for this, Elsa."

"Of course, I am," Elsa said confidently. She hadn't played tennis in years, though, and it showed. When they were done, she was sure she wouldn't be able to walk or move her arms the next day.

"We could make this a thing," Mason said after they were soundly trounced by Ace and DJ in five straight sets.

"If I can walk straight by next Thursday." Elsa panted. "But it was a good workout."

"A couple that plays together stays together," Ace said when he passed them. "Anything I can do to help with the courtship process will be my honor."

"We are not…" Elsa glanced at Mason. "Why aren't you correcting him?"

"Because he is going to think about what he wants, regardless." Mason took her hand and squeezed it, and then released it. She could feel his finger imprint all the way up her arm.

They walked her to her car, and she opened it, standing at the door uncertainly.

"Goodnight, Elsa."

"Night." Elsa murmured huskily.

"I hope that this sweaty session will make you sleep." Mason's voice had a husky timbre to it. "I hope we can do many more sweaty sessions like this in the future."

He had removed his glasses for the game. He had in contacts. Elsa swallowed. "Is that a sexual innuendo?"

Mason laughed and walked closer to her. "Elsa Cara," he picked up the necklace she had around her neck. "You still wear this?"

"Yes," Elsa nodded, the air around them was heightened by tension.

"Good." Mason stepped back. "See you tomorrow."

Elsa nodded. "Yes, see you tomorrow."

Chapter Nineteen

Mason overslept. Oversleeping was so rare that he had to doublecheck his clock before crawling out of bed.

He had the hardest time falling asleep after his tennis match with Elsa. He had a mashup of dreams that involved him running after Elsa, who proved elusive to be caught. It was a long weird dream.

He was still feeling groggy when he walked into the office. Callie looked at him in shock. "It's nine o'clock!"

"I know," Mason mumbled. "Overslept."

"Cameron is waiting for you."

Mason nodded and headed to his office.

Cameron looked at him and grinned. "Torrid night, huh?"

"Yup." Mason nodded.

"Who is she?" Cameron winked. "I won't tell anybody."

"What do you want?" Mason growled. "I am way behind with my day."

"I have him," Cameron said satisfaction lacing his voice.

"I got the juicy goods on Toddy Pryce. It wasn't easy to get this, believe you me, but I find the unfindable."

"What is it?" Mason forced his voice not to sound lackluster. He wasn't feeling the zing of satisfaction that he thought he would feel on hearing that they got Toddy.

"Human trafficking, prostitution… the works."

"He was involved in that?" Mason looked at Cameron incredulously. "Stop pulling my leg. As bad as Toddy Pryce is, he would not do anything like that."

"Not directly," Cameron said, but his nephew Camden owns the nightclub, Jaded. Toddy was an investor and listed as a director in the company. I don't know which smart cookie will make the connection between the Jonathan Pryce that is listed and Toddy Pryce the beloved senator. Jaded, as you know, is under investigation."

"The police are tightening up their case on all of these allegations, but even if they turn out to be untrue, Toddy is toast. Just one leak to the press, and he is a goner. Give me the word. I could leak some salacious things to the press by later today."

"Who else knows about this?" Mason asked.

"No one as yet," Cameron said. "Granted, Toddy doesn't seem to have anything to do with the company, but you know how the news cycle is, you can insinuate and imply and turn public opinion against him. No doubt, the prime minister will ask for his resignation and Toddy will be toast, his reputation will be toast, Even if it is proven that he didn't know a thing about it, his name was attached to this nightclub."

"I'll let you know," Mason had said reluctantly.

"You wanted to sink him," Cameron said, "this is your best bet."

When Cameron left, Mason sat swinging in his chair. Where was his sense of victory? This was bad for Toddy.

Here it was, the revenge he had always sought against Toddy, so why was he so reluctant to pull the trigger?

"Hey Mason, do you have a minute?" Elsa stood in his doorway in a navy blue and white dress, pretty as a picture, with her short curly hair looking a little fluffier than usual, her face flawless and her eyes vulnerable.

Beautiful Elsa, who was always sassy and unafraid and gave as good as she got. She didn't even realize that when she looked at him, it was with the kind of helpless attraction that was probably reflected in his eyes as well. She had always looked at him that way, that look had given him hope through the years that Elsa felt more for him than she allowed him to see.

If he destroyed her brother, he would lose that look directed at him.

"I have a minute." Mason nodded.

"It is about the print copy." She placed some papers on his desk. He approved her work. Inhaling her perfume long after she left. Then he made up his mind to talk to Toddy. Maybe just maybe there was an off chance that Toddy would want to save himself from the judgment about to befall him and that Mason would let him.

He called Myrna to set up an appointment with Toddy for eleven.

****

Toddy's apartment was a far cry from his former home. Mason had not realized how far Toddy had gone to scale down his lifestyle. It was in a small townhouse complex, with only three other houses like it. A small garden was at the front, and there was only a two-car garage.

Myrna greeted him like a long-lost child and escorted him

to Toddy's study, where the once sprightly Toddy was at his desk looking a little worse for wear.

"I know why you are here," Toddy said without preamble and after Myrna had closed the door. "You found out about the nightclub. It was only a matter of time."

Toddy's office had the requisite desk and shelves of books, and it opened onto a covered patio

He stood at the patio doors and looked across at Toddy. "Give me a reason why I shouldn't go to the tabloids with this."

"I'll give you Elsa," Toddy said, "on a platter. Forget about this and stop your vendetta against me."

"Elsa." Mason looked at him incredulously. "Does she know about this?"

"She said she would marry you if you left me alone," Toddy said without preamble.

"Elsa said that?" Mason shook his head and then laughed. "Toddy, you can't give me Elsa. I could have had her if I wanted her years ago, and I can have her now."

Toddy cleared his throat. "I thought…"

"You thought wrong, you are not going to use Elsa as a bargaining chip, and I am not going to even pretend that what you just said is normal," Mason growled. "This is just an example of who you are, bargaining with people."

"You have been a thorn in my father's side for more years than I wanted to count. It ends now, today…one way or the other."

Toddy stood up and braced his hands on the desk. "You don't understand what happened in the past, and I am not going to even bother with the explanation."

"Why not?" Mason asked, "you would prefer to lose your reputation and your senate seat over this."

"I would lose that, but you would lose Elsa too," Toddy

said, "because if you act and destroy her brother, the man who took care of her for all these years, she will not want you anymore. Can you live with that?"

Somehow the thought about losing Elsa was powerful enough to make him pause. "Stop using her as leverage, Toddy! She doesn't belong in this conversation!"

"But she is the only thing I have left to bargain with," Toddy said weakly and then sat down. "I know her. She will not forgive you if you destroy me."

"Maybe I'll risk that." His voice didn't sound as confident, and Toddy's head snapped back, a knowing look in his eyes. "I was right, wasn't I?"

"Right about what?" Mason paced.

"You would forgo this vendetta you have against me for Elsa. She is the key to stopping you," Toddy cackled. "Myrna and your mother know you quite well. Elsa thinks it would be futile. She thinks you wouldn't give up years of misguided revenge for her. She doesn't think you love her enough to put this down."

"Misguided revenge?" Mason raised a brow. That was the only part of Toddy's sentence he wanted to deal with. "There is nothing misguided about what you did to me in the past."

"You have it wrong, Mason," Toddy said tiredly, "so wrong."

"Did you take over my father's company when he died, renamed it, and operated it as your own?"

"Yes," Toddy nodded, "I did, but you got his share of the business, his share of the profits. I preserved it for you. I didn't steal it."

"Didn't you buy his house when he was in a personal financial bind, take over his senate seat, marry his wife, fit yourself into his life?"

"All of those things I had before Manuel Magnus," Toddy

said. "I didn't take over anything."

"What are you saying?" Mason asked, "what on earth are you talking about? You were with my mother before my father?"

"Manuel is the one who wanted everything I had."

"That's a lie!" Mason breathed. He was feeling so angry he felt like punching Toddy. "How dare you say those things about my parents?"

"You don't understand, and I cannot tell you," Toddy said. "I promised your mother. I might have broken all my other promises to her, but this one I keep."

Mason looked at him in frustration. "You are going down."

Toddy said tiredly. "Well, I will wait for the ax to fall."

****

Mason contemplated several times to call Cameron and unleash him on Toddy, but he didn't. He was fuming. The nerve of Jonathan Theodore Pryce to imply that his father was the one who wanted everything he had. Crazy nonsense.

His hand itched to take up the phone and make the call. He called his mother instead.

She answered chirpily as usual. "Hey, honey."

"Were you with Toddy before my dad?" Mason's voice was trembling, "or even during the time when you were married to my dad?"

"Oh, goodness," Celine muttered.

"I have the information to destroy Toddy," Mason gritted out, "I'll do it too."

"I am at home." His mother sighed down the phone. "Come and see me before you do anything rash."

Mason switched lanes and drove to his mother's place as fast as the congested roads would allow.

She was waiting for him at the front door. "I was going to head out to a meeting," Celine said to him sourly. "I had to cancel."

"Thank you for that, I guess." Mason glared at her. He walked into his mother's ultra-modern townhouse. "Am I going to get answers to my questions?"

Celine closed the door behind him and then walked into her open plan living room. "I shouldn't have to tell you anything, Mason. This is all in the past."

"Well, don't tell me," Mason growled. "I'll just give Cameron a call and let him destroy the reputation of your precious Toddy."

"Do you know why Toddy was precious to me?" Celine hissed. "He is the reason why I am who I am. He helped me out when I was younger."

"He bought you an apartment and sent you to school?" Mason looked at his mother, dispassionately. "Were you his mistress?"

"Yes." Celine sat down gingerly on the sofa and clasped her hand one on top of the other. "I am the longest-running mistress that Toddy Pryce ever had. I was with him through wife numbers two and three, and then I became wife number four."

Mason looked at his mother as if he was seeing her for the first time.

"No, I am not proud of it." Celine swallowed. "It wasn't supposed to be like this. I was supposed to marry him after college, but he met a narcissistic woman named Brandy, who trapped him into marriage with a child that wasn't his. She was wife number two, and then there were the children he inherited. I wasn't sure that I wanted to be a mother. When Brandy left, he took his time divorcing her, but I had met Manuel. I decided that I wanted to be a wife."

"So you married him? My father? Was it some kind of sick joke for you?" Mason leaned on the wall, his hand in his pocket.

"No," Celine shook her head, "I tried with your father. I really did. I stayed away from Toddy. He got married to Noreen, and I convinced myself I was happy with Manuel."

"Except you were not." Mason sighed. "You didn't love my father, did you?"

"No." Celine shook her head. "I didn't."

"He loved you, though." Mason ran his hand over his face. "He loved you so much."

"I know." Celine cleared her throat. "Maybe if I hadn't gotten married to him, he would still be alive. I..."

Her voice petered away guiltily. "Your father knew about me and Toddy, that we were lovers for years before I met him, and he got this bee in his bonnet that he was going to compete with Toddy. He tried to outdo Toddy in everything. I don't think he could live down the fact that he married Toddy's mistress."

Celine made a face. "Maybe he thought he was second best. I don't know what went on in his head. He started trying to prove himself. If Toddy said he wanted a senate seat, Manuel wanted one too, and he made it happen, he had more contacts than Toddy. His father was in government."

Mason rubbed his neck. "I can't digest this."

"I know," Celine sighed, "but it has to be said, maybe I should have told you this a long time ago, but you idolized your father, and you were so set against Toddy, and I didn't want my sins of the past to come out. It's not easy confessing to your son that you were not exactly the most upstanding person in your youth."

Mason glared at her. "What would I have done about it, mother? It was in the past, at least I would have known what the lay of the land was instead of assuming stuff that I was clearly wrong about."

"Knowing you, Mason, you would be cold towards me." Celine sighed, "you are my only child. You are all I have."

"Is there more?" Mason gritted out.

Celine nodded. "Well, that house that you accuse Toddy of stealing from your father, Toddy wanted it first, and in his usual petty fashion, your father decided that he was going to have it. He stretched his personal finances by trying to outdo Toddy. It stuck in Manuel's craw when he couldn't make the monthly payments, that is why Toddy got that place at a song.

"Toddy just needed to point out the things he desired, and Manuel would get them for himself in some misguided tit for tat move, and so Toddy started toying with him. He made Manuel get things he didn't even want, and he ran himself into the ground, neglecting his family and his relationships to get these things. That was all on Manuel's head, no one else."

Mason closed his eyes and swallowed. "I can't believe this."

"Yes, well…you are your father's child, you love him, sometimes we can't face the flaws of our parents." Celine sighed, "Manuel, and I didn't have a marriage anymore. We were barely on speaking terms when I started back my relationship with Toddy. I asked him to come over."

Mason's eyes flew open. "What?"

"Yes, I cheated on your father with Toddy. Believe it or not, Toddy was reluctant to be the other man. He didn't like coming to the house, but he made an exception that day. I was crying; it was after a nasty quarrel with Manuel. I am not saying what I did was right. If it makes you feel any better. I got what I deserved when I married Toddy and was at the receiving end of his brand of faithfulness."

"You are no better than Toddy," Mason said harshly. "I can't believe what I am hearing. I am beginning to realize that you deserve each other."

Celine hung her head.

"What happened when you asked Toddy to the house?" Mason asked after a long silence.

"Manuel caught us on camera." Celine sighed, "He had suspected us for some time, and he had hidden cameras in the bedroom."

"Oh no," Mason whispered. "I can't believe this...you caused his heart attack."

"I wouldn't say that," Celine looked at him with tears in her eyes. "Manuel knew about it. He decided to stew about it for weeks before confronting me. He watched the videos over and over again and got angrier and angrier."

"When he finally confronted me about it, I was defiant. He lost it, and we had the mother of all quarrels. He had a heart attack in the middle of a rant."

Mason inhaled, forgetting to release the air in his lungs.

Celine whispered, "Mason, say something."

"You killed my father." Mason finally choked out. "I have been fighting the wrong person all along, haven't I? You and Toddy have been in on this."

"I didn't kill Manuel," Celine said tearfully. "He stressed out himself, worked himself down all because he wanted to one-up Toddy! If Manuel could have just let things go, he would still be alive!"

"Did you know Toddy offered me Elsa in exchange for me not sinking him?" Mason asked.

"Yes!" Celine got up, "I wanted you to choose love over revenge without me having to tell you any of this. I knew that this would hurt."

It did hurt, to his core. He felt like a man bereft. Mason looked down at his hands. He felt deflated. Like all he had held dear was a lie. His version of things had been sorely inaccurate. His father was wronged but not wholly by Toddy.

Some of it was by his own doing, and a large part of it was by his mother who married a man she didn't love.

The complicated love triangle was nauseating. He needed fresh air.

"I'm leaving." Mason stood up.

"Honey," Celine looked at him, her eyes wet. "Please forgive me, I beg you. I don't know how I would survive with you being mad at me."

"You are my mom," Mason said huskily. "I will eventually get around to forgiving, but first, I need to digest all of this."

Celine walked toward him, and he backed away.

"I can't hug you now," Mason said hoarsely.

"What are you going to do about this? Are you going to still pursue this mad revenge against Toddy?" Celine asked, her voice trembling.

"No. It doesn't make any sense," Mason moved away from her and grabbed his car keys from the center table. "Toddy was not the enemy. The enemy was closer to home."

"Mason, no." Celine pleaded. "I was just a young woman who made wrong relationship decisions."

"You played games with my father, and it killed him. I am going to need time to rearrange all of this and put it together before I can move on." Mason headed for the door and then turned and looked at his mother dispassionately. "Give me time to work this out!"

Celine nodded.

He could hear her sobs through the door when he closed it. He swallowed convulsively. He didn't care.

Chapter Twenty

Mason went missing on Monday. He wasn't answering his phones, he had given Callie a terse message that he was unwell and that Elsa was in charge of the Greyson Industries account until he got there.

Elsa was beginning to worry. Mainly because she was suddenly the point man to take over the Greyson Industries new business in his absence. And she was working on a promotion for Heather Greyson's new year charity ball. A task which she had thought would have been a breeze, but she was beginning to realize was a huge production after talking to Heather Greyson's point person.

She felt a little overwhelmed when she heard the grandeur of what she had thought would be a simple ball.

"Toddy Pryce is on the telephone for you," Callie said over the intercom. "And Heather Greyson is on her way over to see you."

"Put Toddy through," Elsa said, panic lacing her voice. She

didn't have a coherent campaign ready for Heather, Toddy was the easiest of the two to deal with.

"Toddy, you have to make this quick," Elsa said, "when she got on the phone, I am doing the job of the man who did the job of two men."

Toddy chuckled. "You can do it. I called to thank you and congratulations."

"Congratulations for what?" Elsa rustled through her papers for the notes she had on Heather Greyson's charity ball, she would have to wing it.

"This morning, Mason called me to apologize." Toddy chirped. "He said he was dropping his vendetta. What on earth did you do? Did you agree to marry him?"

"No, he didn't ask me to marry him," Elsa murmured. "Why is he giving up his revenge?"

"I don't know," Toddy said happily. "Not only is he giving up, but he is also having Cameron Grindley work with me on how to spin the information to the press. What had happened was that I invested in Jaded with Camden…"

"Jaded the sex trafficking club?" Elsa asked in dismay.

"I didn't know anything about that sordid business." Toddy muttered, "I am a victim here."

"Okay, Toddy, I am happy for you," Elsa muttered. "I don't have time for this."

"I'll let you go, thank you for agreeing to be my sacrificial lamb," Toddy said fondly. "I won't forget it."

Elsa looked at the phone, bemused when Toddy hung up. She had all but forgotten that Heather Greyson was on the way. What was going on with Mason? Why had he forgiven Toddy? Had he agreed to marry her? The thought excited her. She got up and sat back down.

She was going to find him if he didn't show up today after she dealt with Heather Greyson.

Heather Greyson entered the office while she was chewing over the questions.

"Ah, hello, Mrs. Greyson," Elsa stood up nervously. The lady was as she remembered: medium height, svelte. Her long wavy hair was dyed a subtle lavender. Just like Florence Jackson. In fact, Heather Greyson looked a little like her.

Elsa smiled at her nervously. "Mrs. Greyson."

"Call me Heather," she smiled at Elsa warmly.

"Have a seat Mrs. Grey...er, Heather."

Heather sat down and looked around. "I like what Mason did with the place. He still keeps photos of the old campaigns on his wall."

Elsa nodded nervously. "I haven't worked on the ball yet; I am just familiarizing myself with the er..."

"I am not here only about the ball," Heather leaned forward. "I am sure Mason must have told you. I mercilessly quizzed him about you and your sisters, the other day. I hope you don't mind."

"I don't mind," Elsa said cautiously. This was the wife of the biggest client in the firm. She didn't want to say the wrong thing.

"Relax Elsa," Heather said, as if reading her mind. "I dropped by just to talk. I have kept up to date with you and your sisters and the Wiley boys."

She laughed. "I can't even call them boys anymore. Ten children all orphaned in the blink of an eye. Your story has stayed with me for years."

"It was tragic." Elsa cleared her throat. "I didn't know you kept up with us."

"I did. I also respect that all ten of you are upstanding citizens, I admire that, and I want to celebrate it. As you know, next year's ball will be at Trident Castle in Portland, I am thinking of calling it back to the beginning."

"I am inviting all the people who meant something to you children. I have been thinking of this for a while, you know."

"You have?" Elsa gasped.

"Oh yes," Heather said dryly. "I consider myself the silent benefactor of you all. Through the years I have done what I could to make things easier for the lot of you while you were growing up. All the Wiley properties were bought at ridiculously low prices. That land that the Wiley Complex is on, we sold to Jordan for a song. He was so excited that he got it at such a low price."

"You were behind it?" Elsa widened her eyes.

"Oh yes," Heather sighed, "when I became aware of you children and your tragedy I had to get involved. We did all our business with Pryceless Advertising because Toddy had you girls. You and your cousins have been my favorite orphans throughout the years."

Elsa cleared her throat, "I don't know what to say."

"Nothing needs to be said. I wish I could have done more." Heather cleared her throat, "Mason told me you discovered new family members recently."

"Yes," Elsa was feeling choked up, and she didn't know why. "We found that we had another aunt named Sara and she has a child, Danica. And I recently found out that I have a grand-aunt, Florence."

"Florence?" Heather's voice trembled a little. "Florence Baxter?"

"Yes, she is Florence Jackson now." Elsa nodded. "She was my grandmother's sister."

"Where is she? I want to meet her," Heather said nervously.

Elsa was confused. "Why would Heather Greyson want to meet Florence Jackson?"

"She lives at Golden Acres, the retirement community in the hills."

"Here in Jamaica?" Heather asked excitedly.

"Yes." Elsa nodded. "Why are you interested in her?"

"I search for family members for others. My charity does this for some of the orphans we work with, in the hopes of a reunion. It's something we like to do. And it was also personal because I met you girls. From the moment I met you and your sisters years ago, I had an instant connection. I wanted to take you to live with me."

"I remember," Elsa said softly. "Maybe you can track down our grandmother, my cousin Danica is obsessed with finding her and Florence too."

"She is?" Heather said softly. "That's sweet of her."

"She is a sweet girl." Elsa cleared her throat, "Mrs. Greyson...Heather..."

Heather looked at her, tears in her eyes. "Oh, Elsa, I know your grandmother, at least I think I do."

"You know her?" Elsa gasped.

Heather held her eyes. "I am her, at least I think I am."

"What?" Elsa froze in her chair. "That's not possible. You are Heather Greyson."

"Previously known as Jane Doe or patient number 11045," Heather said easily. "I was attacked sometime in my past and left on the side of the road to die. How I ended up in Montego Bay. I have no recollection of that event and not much of anything before that either. I was in a coma for close to a year, and when I woke up, I had no memories."

"I gave birth to a child, that much I heard. That child was given away for adoption. I looked for her for years, but I didn't have any real leads. They had my bruised, and battered face splashed all over the place, and nobody claimed me. So I became Jane Doe. The ultimate orphan.

"The doctors kept saying I would recover. Someone would claim me. No one ever did, and I still don't remember anything before waking up in the hospital. It seems as if my memories are gone permanently. I tried a number of treatments to get them back but to no avail. I had to be retaught how to walk and talk and the basics of everything. And though I recovered physically, I am a blank otherwise.

"I met Edmond when I was a patient at in rehab. He had a family member working there, and he visited her once. He took an instant liking to me. He was the one who said I looked like a Heather, not a Jane. When we got married three years later, I became Heather Greyson."

Elsa's mouth was opened, "but how…I have so many questions I don't know where to start. How did you suspect that you were Ivy Baxter Kennedy?"

"I saw you three when you were little tots, Toddy and his partner Manuel Magnus were pitching an idea to my husband, and I saw you playing in the outer offices. I became a little obsessed with you and your story and by extension, the Wiley boys. You children were the inspiration for me to do my charity ball. As I said, you were never far from my mind. I lived in Canada with Edmond for a while, and I never forgot you guys. I always kept in touch, trying to make your lives easier."

"That's awesome." Elsa said in awe, "It's amazing."

"Lately, I have been having dreams." Heather cleared her throat, "I can't see faces I can't remember anything else except the name Florence. The other evening, Mason Magnus told me that you met a new family member named Florence and that her sister abandoned her family. I got to thinking, what are the odds, that it was me."

"Goodness," Elsa whispered. "This is too much."

Heather nodded. "I know I have been thinking the same thing. Maybe Florence can shed some more light on this for me. I am going to visit her today. My driver will take me to

Golden Acres."

Chapter Twenty-One

"**W**here is Mason?" Elsa asked Callie, who was typing up a document at an incredible speed.

Callie looked up at her and still continued to type. "Is something wrong with the Greyson account or the new year's ball? Mrs. Greyson was here for a long time."

"Nothing's wrong with that," Elsa said, "I have to discuss another matter with Mason urgently."

"Okay." Callie nodded. "I guess I can make an exception for you. He said he shouldn't be disturbed."

Elsa waited for Callie to write something else, trying hard not to prompt her.

"He is at Hibiscus Lodge." Callie looked at her with a warning. "You never heard it from me."

"Heard what?"

Elsa left the office at lunchtime.

Mason's car was in the driveway when she drove up. She parked beside it and got out.

Dotty met her at the door.

"Miss Elsa," she smiled broadly. "Mr. Mason is on the upstairs patio meditating."

"Meditating?" Elsa widened her eyes.

"I call it meditating," Dotty said ruefully, "I don't know what else to call it. It's not praying, but this morning, he got up, and he is l philosophical, talking about change and reordering his life. And that nothing is the same anymore. And that you have to trust the process…"

Elsa hurried up the stairs to the outside patio. And there was Mason in a lounge chair with his eyes closed. He was dressed in black track pants; his usually clean-shaven face had the beginnings of a beard.

"Dotty, I am fine, not dying. It is not unusual for people to take a break from everything. I deserve this."

Elsa smiled. He had not even opened his eyes. She pulled up a nearby lounge chair and laid down beside him.

"I completely understand."

Mason's eyes flew open. "Elsa?"

"Yes, it's me. Toddy called me to tell me congratulations. Apparently, you and I are getting married."

Mason chuckled. "He offered you to me, it was something like out of an old movie. I can't believe you agreed to be my prize for giving up my revenge on Toddy."

"He seemed to think it would work, and to be honest, I liked the idea of you choosing me over revenge." Elsa grimaced, "I can't believe it worked."

"It didn't," Mason turned to her. "I didn't appreciate the fact that Toddy was using you as some sort of leverage. Why did you agree to this insanity?"

"Because I…" Elsa cleared her throat, "you want honesty?"

"I always expect it from you." Mason murmured.

"I liked the idea, a little bit, of you choosing me over

revenge. It would be irrefutable proof that you felt something for me." Elsa looked at him. "I have been searching for proof that you felt something for me since I was fifteen, but you never gave a quarter. You are a tough nut to crack. Ace said you were cerebral and not emotional."

"Ace is not a psychiatrist," Mason chuckled, "though he's a little bit right. I like intellectual stimulation, but I inexplicably and without any reason or logic seem to be drawn to you. Besides, if I showed you how I really feel," Mason murmured, "you would not respect me now. You admired my self-control."

"Maybe I did." Elsa snorted. "And maybe I wanted you to act like every other male when he desires a woman, but all of that is in the past. You are going to marry me, aren't you?"

Mason smiled. "Is this a proposal?

"You told Toddy…" Elsa began.

"I told Toddy I was done with revenge, and I apologized to him. My mother set me straight about the past, I now have some facts that I didn't have before. You were right, I should have gotten the back story," Mason sighed. "It was devastating, but it cleared Toddy. I am just licking my wounds in solitude. Slowing it down a bit, digesting the fact that my life or my view of it was a lie."

"Was your mom Toddy's mistress when she was younger? And she married your father in some sort of revenge to make Toddy notice? And then your father knowing the past relationship between the two of them went crazy with trying to outdo Toddy?"

Mason nodded. "Just about. Though you left out the piece where she and Toddy picked up their love affair after that, and my father caught them, and the stress of it killed him."

"I hope you are not blaming her." Elsa gasped. "You are not plotting a new revenge scheme, are you? Against your mom?"

"No, I am done with revenge," Mason said tiredly. "I didn't realize until now how draining it was. I am not blaming my mother or Toddy or my father for anything. That was their drama, I am unsure why I got involved and was so passionate about bringing Toddy down. It seems so pointless now. I am moving on to the next phase."

"Good." Elsa nodded. "I am happy to hear. What is the next phase?"

"Love, a proper relationship, marriage." Mason looked at her. "I am ready for all that it entails. I was never going to be ready with the toxic thoughts I had carrying around and fighting a war with Toddy that I shouldn't have been involved in any way."

"Wow, so I was never in contention for marriage then?" Elsa got up. "This is so embarrassing."

She walked to the patio railing and looked out at the view, but it looked blurry and out of focus. A tear fell on her cheek and then a next one.

Mason wrapped his hand around her and pulled her close into him. "I am happy you came by, Elsa."

"Why?" Elsa choked out.

"Because I did a lot of thinking about us. About our past and our future and…"

"And? Elsa asked breathlessly.

"And no more games," Mason exhaled, "no more secrets. You are smart enough to figure out that you are my fantasy girl, the woman I love. I have given you enough hints for you to pick that up. I want to marry you but not because of some deal your brother cooked up. I want to marry you for you. The sooner, the better."

Elsa turned around, "I love you too, I may have always. I just went about showing it in the wrong way."

"I know." Mason brushed away her tear. "You have the power to crush my heart if you want."

"Never." Elsa moved closer to him. "Perfect love casteth out fear, remember?"

"I remember." Mason kissed her again. "Elsa, will you marry me?"

"Oh, definitely." Elsa murmured on his lips, "definitely."

Chapter Twenty-Two

Nothing could cause such a shockwave in the Wiley/Pryce family than the text that Heather sent Elsa and Elsa sent to the family group.

Heather Greyson wanted to meet all of them at the same place and time.

It was three days since Heather Greyson's DNA test. Everybody had questions.

Walter had invited Elsa over to his place for Sunday brunch and Akeila's birthday party. Akeila was Walter and Aisha's second child, and she was going to be one.

Usually, Elsa avoided the kids parties that happened at the Wiley Complex they seemed to happen so frequently these days especially at this time of the year, every other week there was a party it was becoming hard to keep up, but she figured that this party was going to be special. Even Tiana was hoping to stop by with James. It was turning into a mini family reunion. Walter said he had invited Florence Jackson and Heather Greyson for her to talk to them as she had requested.

So it was going to be little more than a party and a Sunday Brunch. It was a family reunion and a discussion.

Elsa reached the complex a little later than intended. She was not surprised to see that parking before all the houses were taken and the parking lot had few more cars than usual.

Walter greeted her when she alighted from her car. "I was watching for you."

"I wonder why," Elsa hugged him, "what's up?"

"The kids' party is that way," Walter pointed to the common area that was transformed into a castle entrance.

"Princess theme, so common." Walter made a face. "However, Aisha wanted it. So I stepped back, and she did the planning. I think she did a good job, but no way am I going to admit it to her."

Elsa laughed. "You plan Aaron's parties, though." Elsa said, referring to his three-year-old son.

"It's easier, but Aisha is into frills and pinks and girly-girl things for her only daughter. I am told I don't understand. So I let her handle it," Walter said peevishly. "She didn't even ask for my help. She claims that she has picked up a thing or two from me over the years."

"Surely that's not a bad thing," Elsa chuckled, "you can't have the time to be planning parties with so many little Wiley's running around the place. How many Wiley's are there now?"

Walter stopped walking and frowned. "It's not that many of us. Let's see, Preston has two—Pete and Petra. Jordan has two—Courtney and Cairo. I have two—Aaron and Akeila. Saint has two—Sienna and Sara. Guy has one—Joseph Michael. Case has one—Calla Lily, and Pete has Ethan. So that makes it twelve children from the original Wiley brothers. There is one from Pete so far."

"You Wileys are multiplying exponentially." Elsa chuckled. "By next year, there will be even more children. You'll have to plan a party every week, and I'll have to buy my presents in bulk."

"That's not what you do now?" Walter asked, "because that is what I am doing. I can't keep up with parties and such anymore, I am only doing the majors and only by the quarter. The women in the complex have to be taking up the slack, they throw their own parties. I feel envious sometimes, but I am just too busy."

Elsa laughed. "Serves you right."

"Be kind," Walter glared at her, "you are going to want me to plan your wedding. I am very good at that."

"Mason and I haven't discussed wedding plans yet," Elsa said. "He just asked me to marry him this week."

"I know." Walter grinned. "But a little birdie told me it is not going to be a long engagement because Mason has wanted this for a long time."

"This place disperses information faster than social media," Elsa mumbled. "I bet Tiana was the birdie who told you. Tiana is always telling on me."

"I am not giving up my sources," Walter said. "So you really love Mason, don't you?"

"I do, feels like I have loved him forever." Elsa smiled. "It is a relief saying it out loud. I acted like a ninny about it for years."

"I am happy for you," Walter said solemnly.

"Thank you, Walter," Elsa reached into the back of the car for the gaily wrapped present. "Before I forget, I should get the gift."

"You didn't have to get a gift." Walter mused, "the child is just one."

Elsa chuckled. "Of course, I had to get a gift. There was a

gift registry. It made life so much easier."

"Gift registry?" Walter widened his eyes. "There was a gift registry for a one-year-old birthday party. Aisha is stepping this up a whole notch. I had no idea."

"It was the Tiny Tots shop at the Wiley Complex, and it wasn't expensive." Elsa reached into the back for the gift, it was a counting numbers game that the shop clerk had told her was not purchased by anyone else from the Wiley party.

"Leave that for now," Walter said, "we are going to the pool area to meet Heather Greyson. She is not here yet. And we heard that there is a back story here. To say we are all curious is an understatement."

"Okay," Elsa nodded.

"You are the person to give the introductions," Walter said. "We have never met her, and we are all intrigued."

They walked around to the pool area, and Elsa was greeted cheerily by everyone. A sense of anticipation was in the air; she could see that all the Wiley brothers and their wives were there. Florence was in a deep discussion with Jordan when she walked up to the pavilion area and greeted them.

Florence hugged her tightly. "I am so overwhelmed with meeting all of you children. Jordan here tells me that he lived in Dubai for a while. I worked there as a nurse for several years, we could have met each other."

"Okay, everyone." Walter clapped his hands together, "before we head over to the party venue, you have some questions for Elsa. I don't think phone calls or texts were doing it for us."

He turned to Elsa, "The floor is yours, and we are all ears."

Elsa nodded. "There is a back story with Heather Greyson. My sisters and I were featured in a chip advert a long time ago. I think we were about eight."

"We were seven," Tiana said, "I remember because the

year after that I got a bicycle for Christmas and almost broke my arm. I wore a cast when I was eight."

"Thank you," Elsa nodded, "we were taking pictures and posing, and there was this lady behind the scenes watching us. She didn't say much, just stared at us for the two or so hours when we were there."

"And when we were done, she came over and hugged us. I remember her smelling so nice. "

"Yes, I remember." Giselle said, "she had on a bright red and gold sari and bangles all the way up to her left arm."

"That's right." Elsa nodded, "and she said after hugging us. I wish I could take you home with me, but Toddy says no. So what I am going to do is watch out for you. You children had a tough time, didn't you?"

"And she had tears in her eyes," Tiana added. "I remember how she was wiping them away when she left the studio."

"Interesting that she was so emotional about the three of you," Saint said. "I did a preliminary investigation into her, and I found that she is heavily into children's advocacy. She has saved a lot of kids' lives. Her work is amazing."

"She said she looked out for all ten children who were in the tragedy," Elsa said. "She has followed us closely through the years."

"She certainly has," Preston said contemplatively, "I always knew that the land that the Wiley Complex was on was too reasonably priced for it to be a coincidence."

"Yes, the price was pretty low," Jordan added, "I remember remarking to Shawn that I thought the seller had left off one of the zeros."

"I remember," Shawn said. "It was a good deal."

"It was the same with all of my farms," Guy mused aloud. "This Heather lady must have followed my every move. All the lands that I had an interest in buying and actually bought were ridiculously priced even in prime locations. Now I know why."

"She was like a guardian angel," Case mused, "silently watching over us."

There was silence for a while. Everybody mulling over their past good fortunes, sifting through to see if they were linked to Heather Greyson.

"Whoever she is, whether she is my sister or not," Florence said in the silence, "I am grateful to her for taking care of you all."

She had tears in her eyes. "I, for one, am looking forward to knowing if she is my sister after nearly sixty years, this has always been my prayer."

"She is here," Jordan whispered.

"We don't want to overwhelm her," Danica stood up, "I'll go and greet her."

But Heather Greyson wasn't overwhelmed. She was tearful, yes, overjoyed too obviously. She looked around at them, and at Florence and declared, "it seems as if I am biologically related to one Florence Jackson."

"Which means you are our grandmother?" Elsa whispered in the silence.

"I am." Heather nodded. "God does answer prayer, this orphan has finally found her family."

Florence was the first to squeal, hugging Heather tight to her as they cried together.

It was one huge group hug after that as everybody took their turn, hugging Heather and hugging each other, not a dry eye was in the room.

"We may not have had a great beginning," Elsa whispered to Heather when it was her turn to hug, "but this, this is a fabulous end."

The End

Here is an excerpt from Ace
(The Jacksons Book 1)

"I've always thought you would get married before Mason." Ace's aunt, Janet, looked at him slyly. "Not one of Celia's three boys has made it to the altar. I am not implying that there is anything wrong with you, of course. But still…"

She sighed heavily. "Is your brother, Trey, still fooling around with that prostitute?"

Ace inhaled and silently counted to ten. Janet had no filter. She was his mother's oldest sister and the family's busybody, though these days she wasn't as mobile as she used to be, having broken three of her toes in a freak accident involving her cat.

He was the one who had picked the short straw to visit her and check the progress of her healing. His father, Ace Senior, had flatly refused to attend to her because of something Janet said that had caused them to have a falling out. That unfortunately was nothing new.

"I don't know what is going on in Trey's love life at the moment." Ace answered, hoping his voice sounded unbothered.

Janet glanced at him, contemplatively. "I won't even ask about Deuce. Since he broke up with Kelsey he has been drifting through life like a straw at sea. It's quite sad."

"Straw on the sea?" Ace murmured. "I haven't heard that description before."

He unwrapped the bandages and inspected her toes. They were swollen and slightly purple.

"It hurts," Janet groaned. "Am I going to lose my foot?"

"I doubt it," Ace looked at her. "What happened?"

"Someone may have stepped on it at Mason's reception

last night. It was throbbing all night."

"You were told to take better care of them." Ace muttered. "They were almost better."

"But I had to dance with George Brady," Janet fluttered her eyelashes. "He is a lovely man. He can't really dance, and he kept stepping on my poor toes, but I didn't have the heart to tell him to stop."

"Here comes husband number two," Ace chuckled.

"What's wrong with that? Janet mumbled. "He is a widower; I am a widow. Both of us are lonely. The only issue is he doesn't want to live in Kingston, and I am not going back to Portland. I don't like the countryside."

"Well, that is a stalemate—no husband-two for you then." Ace finished dressing her toes and stood up. "You will have to stay off them for at least a week."

"Oh well," Janet shrugged, "that's what you get for having a night of fun. At my age, nights of fun are few and far between. I had to cease it while I could."

"How will you get around the house?" Ace frowned. Janet was a retired music teacher and an empty nester. "Maybe you should ask one of the girls to come by."

"Oh no, "Janet shook her head, her chin-length silver hair glistened in the weak sunlight streaming through her floor to ceiling living room windows. "I love my children and grandchildren, but I prefer them in small, tiny doses and I suspect they feel the same way about me too. I'll be fine. I will hop around. I have my stick and Mavis my housekeeper who comes by three days for the week."

"Okay, if you are sure," Ace packed up his bag and headed to the half bathroom to wash his hands.

"Well, I have a little favor to ask of you, my favorite nephew." Janet hopped to the bathroom door and watched him, "I am renting out the garage apartment. Since Nigel left it has been empty, and I promised George Brady that his daughter could have it. She has been bunking with friends of his and feeling uncomfortable. I have a lovely suite above the garage. She has the privacy, separate entrance, etcetera.

"That's nice." Ace glanced at his aunt as she rambled on. "What's the favor?"

"I would be eternally grateful if you could make sure that everything is in order, show her around. I can't climb the stairs, or you know I would show her around myself. I asked Mavis to thoroughly clean it, so I am sure it is ok. Give her the tour for me, please. I want her to be happy here."

"When is she moving in?" Ace dried his hands and then glanced at his watch. He didn't have anything else to do until five o'clock. Today was supposed to be his lightest day. He usually did his rounds at Golden Acres in the evening.

A car horn blew at the front gate.

"That's her." Janet hopped to the front window and almost tripped over the cat again. She opened the curtain and whistled.

"She has grown into a beauty, but then again, what would one expect from her parentage. She looks a lot like her mom, Charlotte, the harlot. Charlotte slept with anything that could move."

"Aunt Janet," Ace said, warningly, "don't call people names like that."

"It's the truth," Janet snorted, "Charlotte was the Biblical equivalent to Gomer, and George the unfortunate Hosea. Every time that woman strayed he went back for her. The last time he picked her up, she was pregnant and living with Micky Wiley, but George took her back with the pregnancy and gave the child his name and treated her just like his. She's the youngest, but to be honest, I don't think any of the children are even his biologically."

"Did you say Micky Wiley?" Ace stiffened.

"Yup." Janet chortled, "that girl could be Micky Wiley's child. As well as not, who knows. Her mother had a go-around with any man who could walk."

Ace looked through the window at the girl and gasped. She was pretty—cinnamon brown skin, thick curly hair that she had in an unkempt ponytail, perfectly shaped eyebrows, and pink lips. No makeup. She looked fresh-faced and young, slightly puffy around the eyes though as if she hadn't slept for a while. She could be anywhere in her twenties.

"George had her staying with some church friends of his in less than perfect accommodations." Janet murmured. "She looks fresh out of the country and as naïve as a newborn lamb. George kept his girls under tight security and made them dress like destitute nuns. You can understand why he didn't want any of them to be like the mother. You are going to have to keep an eye out for her."

"Me?" Ace whispered. "I don't have any time for that."

"Help your old aunt. I can't do it. I am barely mobile," Janet said. "Show her around. It will take her a while to acclimatize to the place. Kingston is tiny compared to other cities, but it is still a city. She is used to cows and bleating goats and miles and miles of rolling countryside."

"What is her name?" Ace asked.

"Kiya Brady," Janet hopped to the door. "I must greet her; the poor thing looks like she is about to cry."

Ace watched as the taxi man dumped all three of Kiya's bags at her feet. She paid him and then looked at the door again. Janet opened it just in time. Kia slumped her shoulders in relief.

"Hello, dear. Come on up." Janet called from the door. "I am afraid I can't come to help you."

Ace walked behind his aunt, belatedly realizing that he

should offer his assistance. He was so busy looking at Kiya and her obvious relief to be there that he hadn't moved.

"Don't worry about the bags. My nephew will help." Janet smiled. "The neighborhood is fairly good; I doubt they'll rob you in less than a minute."

Ace walked to the door, and his eyes connected with Kiya's, neither of them moved.

"Ace," Janet whispered fiercely under her breath, "don't you dare like that girl. Don't you dare be attracted to this woman."

"Why?" Ace whispered back.

"You know why," Janet said, looking at him meaningfully. "She could be Micky Wiley's daughter and if she is, don't let me say it out loud…"

OTHER BOOKS BY BRENDA BARRETT

Pryce Sisters Series

Baby For A Pryce (Book 1)- Giselle Pryce had a bright future, two scholarships from Ivy League schools and a track career that was going somewhere, when she discovered she was pregnant. She had several decisions to make.

Right Pryce Wrong Time (Book 2)- Tiana got her high school teacher James fired for inappropriate conduct because of her jealousy. When she meets him again as an adult in a different situation, she has no idea how to act.

Yours, For A Pryce (Book 3)- Toddy Pryce offers his favorite sister Elsa to his young political rival Mason Magnus in exchange to not run against him in the next elections.

Wiley Brothers Series

Between Brothers (Book 0)- The beginning of the Wiley brothers saga, Joseph Wiley's unconventional family life may prove to be fatal to some members of the family.

For Pete's Sake (Book 1)- Preston has a run in with a child named Pete who claims that he is the grandson of their former housekeeper Pamela Stone.

Crossing Jordan (Book 2)- Jordan is miffed when Shawn takes her new fiancé to Jamaica and insists that he be man of honor at their wedding.

Fire and Walter (Book 3)- Walter's past came rushing to greet him shortly after his appointment as church elder. The new pastor was his childhood molestor, his wife was his ex from college and her cousin was the girl who got away. Walter had a lot of decisions to make.

The Perfect Guy (Book 4) - After a patient five years waiting for Lucia, Guy had his work cut out for him to prove himself worthy of her affections. He had played the part of poor farmer for too long and now he had competition in the form of the handsome doctor Ace Jackson.

The Patience of A Saint (Book 5)- Something was wrong with Saint's wife Sandrene. It didn't take a genius to see that she was changed beyond all recognition. Saint had to get to the bottom of it, before it was too late for them to salvage anything from the relationship.

A Case of Love (Book 6)- After a concert, Case is offered a girl to buy. Her fate was in his hands. He could keep her or leave her to the mercy of her evil family.

Resetter Series

Never Too Late (Book 1)- Addi finds out she is a resetter and goes back to the summer of 92 to change her family's lives.

Never Say Never (Book 2)- Skyler's handsome college lecturer, who happens to be her neighbor, has a 't' in his palms. Should she tell him the significance of it. If she does, would he believe her?

Now or Never (Book 3)- Ten years later Addi and Randy meet again at Randy's engagement party. Why is it that the chemistry between them was still so potent? Can they ever have a future together? Would Randy choose her this time around?

Almost Never (Book 4)- Tech genius Joshua Porter had all but given up on love. He then meets Portia, an inmate at the female penitentiary and his life takes a turn for the adventurous.

The Scarlett Family Series

Scarlett Baby (Book 1)- When the head of the Scarlett family died, Yuri had to return home to Treasure Beach for the funeral. What he didn't count on was seeing Marla, his childhood sweetheart and his best friend's wife. And when emotions overwhelm them and a few months later Marla is pregnant, Yuri wants the impossible: his best friend's wife and the baby they made together...

Scarlett Sinner (Book 2)- Pastor Troy Scarlett realizes the hard way that some sins are bound to be revealed, like the child that he had out of wedlock with his wife's mortal enemy from college. His wife Chelsea was not happy with the status quo. She was not taking care of the son of the woman she had so despised from college. And she could not get over the deep betrayal that she felt from her husband's indiscretion.

Scarlett Secret (Book 3)- Terri Scarlett had a soft spot for her friend, Lola. She was funny and sweet and they looked remarkably alike. But when Lola's Arab prince demands his bride, Terri foolishly exchange places with her friend and they meet up on a world of trouble.

Scarlett Love (Book 4)- Slater always looked forward to delivering packages to the law firm where he could get a glimpse of the stunning female lawyer, Amoy Gardener. Unfortunately, for Slater a woman like Amoy would not take him seriously, especially when she found out that he could not read!

Scarlett Promise (Book 5)- Driven by desperation Lisa Barclay decides to make some extra money by prostituting herself after being kicked out in the streets. Her first customer turns out to be a popular government senator and then to her horror he dies...

Scarlett Bride (Book 6)- When Oliver Scarlett's missionary work in the Congo region was coming to an end, he had a decision to make, marry Ashaki Azanga and save her from being the fourth wife to the chief of the village or leave her to her fate and get on with his life...

Scarlett Heart (Book 7)- After receiving a heart transplant shy librarian Noah Scarlett started to take on character traits that were unlike him and he kept dreaming of a girl named Cassandra Green...

Rebound Series

On The Rebound- For Better or Worse, Brandon vowed to stay with Ashley, but when worse got too much he moved out and met Nadine. For the first time in years he felt happy, but then Ashley remembered her wedding vows...

On The Rebound 2- Ashley reinvented herself and was now a first lady in a country church in Primrose Hill, but her obsessed ex friend Regina showed up and started digging into the lives of the saints at church. Somebody didn't like Regina's digging. Someone had secrets that were shocking enough to kill for...

Magnolia Sisters

Dear Mystery Guy (Book 1)- Della Gold details her life in a journal dedicated to a mystery guy. But when fascination turns into obsession she finds herself wanting to learn even more about him but in her pursuit of the mystery guy she begins to learn more about herself...

Bad Girl Blues (Book 2)- Brigid Manderson wanted to go to med school but for the time being she was an escort working for her mother, an ex-prostitute. When her latest customer offers her the opportunity of a lifetime would she take it? Or would she choose the harder path and uncertain love with a Christian guy?

Her Mistaken Dreams (Book 3)- Caitlin Denvers dream guy had serious issues. He has a dead wife in his past and he was the main suspect in her murder. Did he really do it? Or did Caitlin for the first time have a mistaken dream?

Just Like Yesterday (Book 4)- Hazel Brown lost six months of memory including the summer that she conceived her son, and had no idea who his father could be. Now that she had the means to fight to get him back from the Deckers, she finds out that the handsome Curtis Decker is willing to share her son with her after all.

New Song Series

Going Solo (Book 1)- Carson Bell, had a lovely voice, a heart of gold, and was no slouch in the looks department. So why did Alice abandon him and their daughter? What did she want after ten years of silence?

Duet on Fire (Book 2)- Ian and Ruby had problems trying to conceive a child. If that wasn't enough, her ex-lover the current pastor of their church wants her back...

Tangled Chords (Book 3)- Xavier Bell, the poor, ugly duckling has made it rich and his looks have been incredibly improved too. Farrah Knight, hotel heiress had cruelly rejected him in the past but now she needed help. Could Xavier forgive and forget?

Broken Harmony(Book 4)- Aaron Lee, wanted the top job in his family company but he had a moral clause to consider just when Alka, his married ex-girlfriend walks back into his life.

A Past Refrain (Book 5)- Jayce had issues with forgetting Haley Greenwald even though he had a new woman in his life. Will he ever be able to shake his love for Haley?

Perfect Melody (Book 6)- Logan Moore had the perfect wife, Melody but his secretary Sabrina was hell bent on breaking up the family. Sabrina wanted Logan whatever the cost and she had a secret about Melody, that could shatter Melody's image to everyone.

The Bancroft Family Series

Homely Girl (Book 0) - April and Taj were opposites in so many ways. He was the cute, athletic boy that everybody wanted to be friends with. She was the overweight, shy, and withdrawn girl. Do April and Taj have a love that can last a lifetime? Or will time and separate paths rip them apart?

Saving Face (Book 1) - Mount Faith University drama begins with a dead president and several suspects including the president in waiting Ryan Bancroft.

Tattered Tiara (Book 2) - Micah Bancroft is targeted by femme fatale Deidra Durkheim. There are also several rape cases to be solved.

Private Dancer (Book 3) Adrian Bancroft was gutted when he returned to Jamaica and found out that his first and only love Cathy Taylor was a stripper and was literally owned by the menacing drug lord, Nanjo Jones.

Goodbye Lonely (Book 4) - Kylie Bancroft was shy and had to resort to going to confidence classes. How could she win the love of Gareth Beecher, her faculty adviser, a man with a jealous ex-wife in his past and a current mystery surrounding a hand found in his garden?

Practice Run (Book 5) - Marcus Bancroft had many reasons to avoid Mount Faith but Deidra Durkheim was not one of them. Unfortunately, on one of his visits he was the victim of a deliberate hit and run.

Sense of Rumor (Book 6) - Arnella Bancroft was the wild,

passionate Bancroft, the creative loner who didn't mind living dangerously; but when a terrible thing happened to her at her friend Tracy's party, it changed her. She found that courting rumors can be devastating and that only the truth could set her free.

A Younger Man (Book 7)- Pastor Vanley Bancroft loved Anita Parkinson despite their fifteen-year age gap, but Anita had a secret, one that she could not reveal to Vanley. To tell him would change his feelings toward her, or force him to give up the ministry that he loved so much.

Just To See Her (Book 8)- Jessica Bancroft had the opportunity to meet her fantasy guy Khaled, he was finally coming to Mount Faith but she had feelings for Clay Reid, a guy who had all the qualities she was looking for. Who would she choose and what about the weird fascination Khaled had for Clay?

The Three Rivers Series

Private Sins (Book 1)- Kelly, the first lady at Three Rivers Church was pregnant for the first elder of her church. Could she keep the secret from her husband and pretend that all was well?

Loving Mr. Wright (Book 2)- Erica saw one last opportunity to ditch her single life when Caleb Wright appeared in her town. He was perfect for her, but what was he hiding?

Unholy Matrimony (Book 3) - Phoebe had a problem, she was poor and unhappy. Her solution to marry a rich man was derailed along the way with her feelings for Charles Black, the poor guy next door.

If It Ain't Broke (Book 4)- Chris Donahue wanted a place in his child's life. Pinky Black just wanted his love. She also wanted him to forget his obsession with Kelly and love her. That shouldn't be so hard? Should it?

Contemporary Romance/Drama

After The End--Torn between two lovers. Colleen married her high school sweetheart, Isaiah, hoping that they would live happily ever after but life intruded and Isaiah disappeared at sea. She found work with the rich and handsome, Enrique Lopez, as a housekeeper and realized that she couldn't keep him at arms length...

Love Triangle: Three Sides To The Story- George, the husband, Marie, the wife and Karen-the mistress. They all get to tell their side of the story.

The Preacher And The Prostitute - Prostitution and the clergy don't mix. Tell that to ex-prostitute, Maribel, who finds herself in love with the Pastor at her church. Can an ex-prostitute and a pastor have a future together?

New Beginnings - Inner city girl Geneva was offered an opportunity of a lifetime when she found out that her 'real' father was a very wealthy man. Her decision to live up-town meant that she had to leave Froggie, her 'ghetto don,' behind. She also found herself battling with her stepmother and battling her emotions for Justin, a suave up-towner.

Full Circle- After graduating from university, Diana

wanted to return to Jamaica to find her siblings. What she didn't foresee was that she would meet Robert Cassidy and that both their pasts would be intertwined, and that disturbing questions would pop up about their parentage, just when they were getting close.

Historical Fiction/Romance

The Empty Hammock- Workaholic, Ana Mendez, fell asleep in a hammock and woke up in the year 1494. It was the time of the Tainos, a time when life seemed simpler, but Ana knew that all of that was about to change.

The Pull Of Freedom- Even in bondage the people, freshly arrived from Africa, considered themselves free. Led by Nanny and Cudjoe the slaves escaped the Simmonds' plantation and went in different directions to forge their destiny in the new country called Jamaica.

Jamaican Comedy (Material contains Jamaican dialect)

Di Taxi Ride And Other Stories- Di Taxi Ride and Other Stories is a collection of twelve witty and fast paced short stories. Each story tells of a unique slice of Jamaican life.

www.ingramcontent.com/pod-product-compliance
Lightning Source LLC
Chambersburg PA
CBHW050734230626
47052CB00002BA/179